SUZANNAH ROWNTREE

Ten Thousand Thorns

Second edition

Cover art by rebecacovers
Editing by Lucinda Holdsworth

This book was professionally typeset on Reedsy.
Find out more at reedsy.com

My warmest thanks to Steven Wei for helping me get the details right.
Needless to say, any mistakes that remain are completely my fault.

Chapter 1.

I n Hubei, there was a bamboo forest.

In the bamboo forest was a tavern.

In the tavern was a traveller who did not show his face.

He sat in the darkest corner of the room with his head bent, so that as she poured his tea, the taverner's daughter was only able to catch a glimpse of a chin beneath his hood. On the table before him lay a long box of dark, polished teak-wood, carved with tigers.

"Thank you," he said, reaching forward to pick up the bamboo cup. The taverner's daughter straightened, clasping the teapot to her chest.

"Are you travelling far, Elder?"

He sipped his tea and replaced it on the table before replying.

"Wudang Mountain."

Although the traveller spoke softly in the crowded tavern, his words caused a hush. At a table nearby, an unremarkable little man with streaks of grey in his hair and squinted eyes that had almost vanished into the broad planes of his face turned almost imperceptibly and tried to see the face under the hood. The taverner's daughter adopted a more respectful tone at once.

"If Elder is headed to Wudang, he should be careful! The Emperor has beheaded Duke Roaring Tiger in Nanjing; his head has been sent around the eight directions. Now the Mount Jing rebels have no leader, and they are like swarming hornets or wounded bears. If Elder travels by the south road, he may find himself entangled. Take the north road to Wudang instead."

The traveller thanked her with a nod. At the next table, the little man looked at the teapot and cleared his throat, hoping for the girl's attention.

But she didn't hear him.

Outside the tavern, a voice screamed. The sound of racing footsteps came closer. Closer.

And then—

Poom.

The body of a man burst through the wall of the tavern in a shower of flying splinters. The hooded traveller snatched up the wooden box and jumped to his feet as the body landed on the table before him with a crash. The table collapsed. Inside the tavern, chaos reigned. As the taverner's daughter screamed, some felt for weapons, while others scrambled away in fear.

Lit up by the glare of the evening sun, the traveller stood above the wreck of his table, his arm stretched out, the wooden box trembling in his hand. For a brief moment,

2

everyone in the tavern saw his face—a young face, a noble face, with high cheekbones and watchful eyes.

A shadow hid him again.

A black silhouette stepped through the large jagged hole in the tavern's wall. Once inside the newcomer straightened, revealing beneath a woven reed hat the features of a young maiden as fair and as delicate as a piece of white jade. The traveller blinked in disbelief. Surely, this could not be the one who had blasted such an immense hole in the wall? He was amazed to hear the gasps of terror from those around him.

"It's Tie Niang", someone cried, "the Iron Maiden!"

Iron Maiden smiled gently, kicked aside a loose plank and settled herself at an empty table.

"Is that tea?" she asked the taverner's daughter in a voice as small and gentle as she herself appeared.

The girl crept forward with her teapot, and filled a cup for Iron Maiden. Her hands shook, and a few drops from the spout spattered the table. No one moved or spoke as Iron Maiden shook back her ragged sleeve and lifted her cup. After one sip she grimaced and tossed the contents out. "Ugh! Bitter as a winter's night. Do you call that tea?"

The taverner's daughter let out a terrified sob.

"Never mind, I'll make my own." Iron Maiden fished inside her bag and brought out a tiny tea caddy delicately painted with white cranes. At the sight of it, the silence within the tavern grew yet more profound. Iron Maiden

3

was dressed like a peasant, but perhaps she was of higher status than she appeared.

Or perhaps she had fought someone important and stolen their tea.

"I'll bring hot water, miss!"

The taverner's daughter fled.

Amidst the wreckage of the broken table, there came a soft groan from the man who had entered by the wall, a venerable old peasant with white hair and long grey robes. Now, he tried to rise from his undignified position. Quickly the traveller put his foot on the old man's chest, pushing him back down to the floor and shaking his head, but it was already too late. The movement had attracted Iron Maiden's attention. With a sigh, she tucked the tea back into her bag, then stood up and bowed to everyone inside the tavern, her right fist held cupped in her left hand.

"Tomorrow at dawn, I will be waiting outside the Temple of Tranquil Longevity to exchange stances with your martial artists!"

Despite the traveller's warning, the old man rose shakily to his feet and tottered toward the opening in the broken wall. At once Iron Maiden pounced on him and sealed an acupoint on his neck. The old man slumped, unconscious.

"I am taking this man with me," she announced. "If you want him back, send your greatest martial artists to me without fail at dawn tomorrow!"

With that, she grabbed the old man by the scruff of his neck and flitted through the jagged hole in the wall. Despite the burden of her captive, she moved as lightly as a dandelion seed blowing on the wind. For a moment she could be glimpsed flying through the village like a swooping crane or a soaring dragon, until she reached the bamboo forest and vanished into its depths.

The traveller took a deep breath. If he hadn't seen it with his own eyes, he would never have believed that such a profound lightness skill was possible.

As soon as the Iron Maiden had departed, the tavern filled with cries of outrage.

"This Iron Maiden must be stopped," someone wailed. "First she terrorises Peaceful Settlement, Prosperous Settlement, and Fortunate Settlement—and now she has kidnapped our own village chief! Is there no limit to her arrogance?"

"Why would she pick on a harmless old man?"

"He was only putting up the imperial edict."

A young man in the blue clothes of a ninth-rank official came in by the door. He held a torn, dirty piece of woodblock-printed paper close to his eyes in the failing light.

"We just received these today. 'By order of the Vastly Martial Emperor. Wanted for rebellion and treason, the bandit Clouded Sky, associate and aide to the disgraced Roaring Tiger. Last seen in Nanjing; thought to be travelling to Wudang Mountain. For information leading to Clouded Sky's arrest, two thousand gold taels.'

The taverner's daughter peeked out from her hiding-place in the kitchen, still clasping her pot of bitter tea. She squeaked, "The Iron Maiden is one of the Roaring Tiger rebels?"

"No! She's just a troublemaker trying to prove herself supreme in the martial arts world!"

"My poor uncle," the taverner's wife began to sob.

"There must be *someone* who can face the Iron Maiden." The official handed the edict to the taverner's daughter and turned to a man sitting at a nearby table. "You, Old White Rabbit?"

"Me? No! She has already defeated a dozen martial artists stronger than me!"

"Send for Black Jade Madame!"

"Haven't you heard? Black Jade Madame was defeated by Iron Maiden last month! She may not have recovered from her injuries yet!"

"I heard that Snow Wind was seen in Hubei within the last week."

"Snow Wind? With the Venomous Knives? We can't ask him for help," said Old White Rabbit. "His martial arts are profound, but unorthodox! He could deal with Iron Maiden, but what if he turned on us after?"

"Besides, he has a commission from the Emperor now." The official gestured toward the edict. "He's busy hunting Clouded Sky."

A desolate silence fell. The little man with the unre-

6

markable face stole another glance at the hooded traveller. He had sunk back onto his seat, holding the wooden box across his knees, his head bent as though his mind was far away.

The taverner's daughter looked up from the imperial edict.

"Everyone knows that Wudang Sect is unparalleled in the martial arts community." She crossed the room and dropped the edict on the floor at the traveller's feet. Printed upon it was a young, noble face with high cheekbones and watchful eyes. Softly, she said: "Do you, Elder, know anyone who will fight Iron Maiden for us?"

The traveller closed his eyes, knowing that all eyes in the tavern were on him. A murmur ran around the room as first one, then another recognised him as the fugitive whose face was printed on the edict. He had come so far. He was so close to home. If he turned aside now, what would happen to his people? What would happen to Hubei? For the sake of the greater good, he ought to refuse. But he was a martial artist. And every martial artist knew that it was his personal duty to do justice, to help the needy, and to rely with humility upon Heaven.

The young girl's lips tightened in determination.

"If you help us, you can rely on us not to turn you in, Elder."

But only if he helped them. He could read the threat in not only her eyes, but also in those of all others inside the tavern. Now that they had seen his face and heard of the

7

reward, there was only one way to make sure he returned to Wudang in safety.

The traveller picked up the imperial edict and stood.

"Yes," he said. "I am Wudang disciple Clouded Sky, third-in-command to Duke Roaring Tiger. If you will not betray me to the Emperor, then I will fight Iron Maiden and free your chief."

* * *

The little man with the unremarkable face slipped out of the tavern into the dusk. For a short time he stood quietly in the street listening to the sounds of the village as it settled in for the night. He saw no reason to fear danger. No dark shapes flitted over the grey rooftops; no glint of steel shone in the shadows. Abruptly, he turned east.

Not far from the village he left the road and threaded his way through the forest. It was even darker under the canopy, and he saw the glow of the campfire long before he reached it.

He could just make out voices when someone challenged him from the shadows.

"Who goes there?"

"My name is Second Brother. I've come to speak to the Imperial Sword."

It seemed that this was the wrong answer. The guard in the shadows drew his sword and leaped. A muffled blow connected, then another.

Second Brother took the unconscious guard by the scruff of his neck and dragged him noisily through the fallen leaves, down toward the hollow beyond. About thirty men, all wearing the red and black livery of the Vastly Martial Emperor, jumped to their feet with shouts of alarm when they saw Second Brother and his prisoner.

"I've come to speak to the Imperial Sword," Second Brother repeated, aiming a fist at his prisoner's death acupoint. The guards froze, their sabres half unsheathed.

"Your excellency," one of them whispered.

Next to the fire sat a man wearing the purple silk that only officials of the highest rank were permitted to wear. Across his knees lay a sword with a silken yellow tassel. An imperial sword. The personal authorisation of the Emperor himself. His face was covered by a black muffler that left only his eyes visible—and even those were closed in meditation.

"Your excellency," the guard hissed more urgently.

The Imperial Sword spoke without opening his eyes. "Falling leaves may disturb the surface, but deep down, do the fish waken?"

A faint smile creased Second Brother's eyes.

"They do if they're hungry."

The Imperial Sword opened his eyes.

"Who are you?"

"Merely a peasant who wants to help, your excellency." The Imperial Sword looked thoughtfully at the guard

9

lying motionless among the tawny-coloured leaves at Second Brother's feet.

"A martial artist of your stature need not call himself a mere peasant. What have you come to offer?"

"Information, your excellency. Tomorrow morning at dawn, if you go to the Temple of Tranquil Longevity, you'll find the one you're looking for."

"I expect you want something in return for this."

Second Brother shook out the imperial edict, revealing the printed face of Clouded Sky.

"Two thousand taels is a lot of money. Even part of such a sum would be a fortune to someone like me."

The Imperial Sword considered him for a long moment.

"Perhaps we can come to an agreement," he said at last.

* * *

The Temple of Tranquil Longevity stood halfway up a mountain, shrouded by mists and conifers. Not long ago, ten Taoist priests lived here. But when the Vastly Martial Emperor began to subdue Hubei Province, he forced the priests to leave their temple and travel in ten different directions so that they could no longer discuss seditious ideas together. His soldiers had taken the books, stripped the gold and silver, and left the temple to decay, its carvings chipped and the red tiles of its double roof clouding over with lichen.

Clouded Sky reached the high ledge of the mountain temple and waited for a little while to catch his breath. It had been a long climb, but he could not afford to waste his reserves of *qi* energy by using his *Cloud-Ascending Ladder* lightness skill to flit up the mountain.

He loosened his black sword in its sheath and made sure that the carved wooden box was strapped securely to his back. There was no sign of the Iron Maiden outside the temple, but as Clouded Sky climbed the broken steps, he saw what looked like a small grey bundle lying between the carved pillars in front of the open doors. The village chief.

Clouded Sky squinted into the shadowed interior and drew his sword.

A voice spoke, its echoes rippling sweetly around the empty chamber. "So, they found someone to fight me! Good!"

Clouded Sky frowned into the darkness, but still, he could see no one. Cautiously, he reached down with his left hand and held it in front of the old man's nose. Breath warmed his fingers. The chief was still alive.

"The Cloud Gate acupoint," said Iron Maiden from inside the temple. "Unseal it and let him go. Now that you are here I am quite satisfied."

Clouded Sky jabbed the acupoint, and the chief awoke with a start.

"Hero!" he rasped, grabbing Clouded Sky's arm. "Be careful! It's Miss Iron!"

"Boo!" said the voice in the temple, and laughed.

"I know," said Clouded Sky. "I came to exchange stances with her!"

He tried to stand, but the old man tightened his grip, his eyes widening. "I know you! You are Clouded Sky!"

"Don't speak so loud, Elder," Clouded Sky begged, but another laugh drifted out of the temple.

"Clouded Sky! Fortunate meeting, fortunate meeting. A Wudang Sect warrior reputed for skill and courage!" There was a flutter of fabric within the temple as Iron Maiden jumped down from the rafter where she had perched. She landed lightly and bowed with cupped fists. "It is a privilege to exchange stances with you, hero!"

The chief hastily bowed before hurrying away toward the path down the mountain. Clouded Sky straightened with a grim smile, lifting his sword to point at Iron Maiden.

"You have not fought a Wudang Sect disciple before?"

She shrugged. "Your Wudang Sect is too arrogant. You are the first to agree to exchange stances with me."

"Perhaps I should not give you face by agreeing to exchange stances now."

"Too late for that! You are here now, and I won't let you leave without a fight!" With a quick motion of each hand, she wrapped the ends of her sleeves around her fists.

"As you wish." Clouded Sky took a stance from Wudang Sect's one hundred-stroke Mystical Sword Style. "It's the duty of every righteous warrior to punish injustice!"

Iron Maiden leaped into the air. Her lightness skill was incredible: she soared through the shadows of the temple like a meteor, her feet lashing out at him with a speed and power he was unprepared to face. Clouded Sky lifted his sword, blocking her kicks, but the impact blasted him backward.

Poom!

He flew through the air, staggering backwards as he landed on the grassy clearing in front of the temple.

Iron Maiden instantly leaped to attack again, this time with her fists. Clouded Sky knew better now than to block her strokes. Instead he gave way, dodging aside and aiming his blade at her Soul Gate acupoint, using the stance *Ambush From Ten Directions*. The blade flickered with impossible speed, but Iron Maiden blocked it with a simple palm strike.

Boom!

Once more the force of the two strokes meeting each other threw them apart, propelling them to opposite sides of the clearing.

"Your Wudang Sword Skill is impressive!" Iron Maiden called from the shadows of the trees opposite. "I've rarely seen a blade move so fast!"

Clouded Sky was just as astonished by Iron Maiden's *qi* cultivation and internal force. He had owned his sword since the age of ten, practicing with it faithfully each day for hours. By now it held its own *qi* energy. It should have been impossible to block, yet Iron Maiden had blocked

13

it.

Now she stood on the opposite side of the clearing, smiling at him like a *shifu* applauding his disciple for a lucky stroke. Frowning, Clouded Sky adopted another stance. This time, he attacked.

Iron Maiden saw him coming and flitted toward him, the force of her palm strikes kicking up clouds of dust as she approached. Under the ferocity of her attack, Clouded Sky was compelled to take a defensive stance once again. Blow after blow rained upon him as she targeted his acupoints, moving almost too fast to see. Clouded Sky defended until his sword seemed to form a flickering black shield around him, but still she pressed forward.

The intensity and speed of Iron Maiden's attack would have destroyed anyone else's defences within moments, but as Clouded Sky retreated he began to understand and even predict her movements. Good—he only had to keep up his defence until her energy failed enough to let him strike. Step by step, he retreated across the grass, his confidence gradually mounting. Now she used *Iron Monkey Climbs the Stair*. Now she attacked with *Broken String of Pearls*. Next, he realised with part of his mind that was moving too fast for words, she would use *Fortunate Palms of Dragon Gate*. And then he would have her in the brief moment when she left an acupoint on her flank unguarded.

He lunged—but his sword missed her. It was the stance

14

he had expected, but instead of using it defensively, she employed it to launch an attack. And with his own sword at full extension, Clouded Sky was completely defenceless.

The force of her palm caught his left shoulder and hurled him spinning through the air toward the edge of the clearing.

With a hastily-thrown kick, Clouded Sky saved himself from slamming into a tree, then landed on his feet. Ready to collapse, he leaned against the tree, gasping for air.

"Who—who is your *shifu?*" he panted.

Iron Maiden dropped her stance and stepped back, wiping the hair out of her eyes. "My *shifu?* Why do you want to know my *shifu?*"

"Because I recognise that skill! That is a variation of Wudang Sect's Heaven-Shaking Iron Palm Technique! How did you learn it?"

She shook her head. "I didn't know that was its name."

"You must have been taught by some heretic." That would explain that last, terrible, unpredictable palm strike. Clouded Sky shivered. As a young girl, Iron Maiden was physically weaker than a man, so all her palm strikes had to be augmented with her internal force to a much greater degree. It must be taking a terrible toll on her, yet she appeared not to feel it. She must have vast reserves of *qi* to draw on. Combined with an unorthodox palm technique, that made her far more dangerous than he had imagined.

For the first time, Clouded Sky feared he might actually

lose this duel. The whole Wudang Sect would lose face—and it would be his fault.

"A heretic?" For a moment Iron Maiden looked aghast, but she quickly shook her head. "I don't believe that! Just because you don't understand my martial arts doesn't make them unorthodox."

"You, Miss Iron, would have been well advised to learn the *real* Heaven-Shaking Iron Palm Technique. Your palm was off-target."

"Of course it was off-target, otherwise I would have seriously hurt you! But who was *your shifu?* He has some explaining to do."

"What do you mean?"

"Your sword style is faulty, hero! When it should attack, instead it defends. How can you win any fights using such a style?"

Clouded Sky frowned, his hand tightening on the hilt of his weapon. "Faulty? This is Wudang Sect's Mystical Sword Style!"

She shook her head. "It is ineffective. Your *shifu* must be afraid you will one day surpass him. Or turn against him."

Clouded Sky tried to rein in his outrage at the offence. Only an ignorant peasant would speak of another martial artist's *shifu* so disrespectfully.

"It is customary for masters to conceal part of what they know."

She laughed. "That's why All-Under-Heaven is in the

state it is today!"

"How dare you!" Clouded Sky levelled his sword at Iron Maiden. "Fine, I'll show you whether I can attack!"

He launched himself toward her, attacking from above using *Taishan Pressing Down the Apex*. At once, Iron Maiden flitted aside. Clouded Sky expected her to counter with a diagonal attack to his lower body. For a moment, it seemed that this was what she was doing, but instead she performed a flip in the air. One of her feet flashed out and hit an acupoint on the side of his neck. Clouded Sky's body immediately locked in place, sword arm extended stiffly before him. With the acupoint sealed, his *qi* could no longer flow freely. His head buzzed with pain. Back on her feet, Iron Maiden put a hand to her mouth.

"Oh no! I didn't know I could do that. I was going to let you show me, I promise."

Was she *mocking* him now? But Clouded Sky didn't have time for anger. From where he stood immobile he noticed the tall conifers growing on the hillside beginning to wave as if stirred by a strong wind.

But there was no wind.

"Don't worry about losing face, hero," Iron Maiden said. "I won't tell anyone I defeated you in one stance."

Incredibly, she seemed sincere. But at this moment he wasn't worried about face. More and more of the trees began to wave. A flash of light came from one deep within the forest. Blades! Clouded Sky summoned all

17

his energy, but only a strangled sound escaped his throat. Iron Maiden took no notice.

"What are you carrying, hero?" She reached behind Clouded Sky's back and pulled the wooden box from his shoulders. "You've been taking good care of this, I can tell."

The trees shuddered, and Clouded Sky saw a glimpse of colour. Black and red—Imperial guards! Someone from the tavern must have talked. He attempted to calm his mind enough to summon the internal force required to unlock the sealed acupoint, but it was useless. He was too agitated.

Still oblivious to the approaching danger, Iron Maiden slid open the carved box. She reached inside and lifted up a short truncheon with a blade mounted on the end and a tassel of white silk.

"A broken spear?" She lifted a quizzical eyebrow at him.

Behind her, the trees shook wildly.

As Iron Maiden looked into the mirror-bright spear blade her eyes widened. She struck Clouded Sky's acupoint and turned in the same motion, whirling the broken spear before her. Not a moment too soon. Two flying daggers hummed from the trees.

"The beastly Emperor!" Iron Maiden swatted the deadly blades aside and launched herself into the air.

The imperial guards shouted as they leaped from the treetops, cleaving the air with spears and sabres.

Clouded Sky stomped on the weapon-box Iron Maiden had dropped, flipping it into his left hand. He had just enough time to sling it over his shoulders. Then the guards were on him.

For a moment, Clouded Sky wondered if he was as poor a martial artist as Iron Maiden seemed to think. How would he stand up to the Emperor's highly-trained guards? But to his relief, he found that none of them had a skill like his. Clouded Sky's sword was faster than sight, and his Wudang Sect Mystical Sword Style made an impenetrable defense around him. Quickly, he burst through their encirclement.

Closer to the trees, Iron Maiden fought a ring of guards, attacking with her right palm and defending with the broken spear in her left hand. With most of the Emperor's men busy fighting her, Clouded Sky could take this opportunity to slip down the mountain, mount his horse, and ride away.

But that would mean losing the spear.

He pelted toward Iron Maiden as two more daggers flew from the treetops. Not breaking stride, Clouded Sky deflected them into the fight before him.

They sank into the acupoints of two combatants, who collapsed with howls of pain. Clouded Sky leaped over their bodies and landed beside Iron Maiden. Quickly, the rest of the guards encircled them. Back to back, Clouded Sky and Iron Maiden waited for them to charge. Instead, a black-clad swordsman leaped from the treetops, soaring through the air to land effortlessly before them. He wore a hood and mask, but the sword in his hand bore a yellow tassel.

The Imperial Sword's voice was a hoarse whisper. "A righteous hero doesn't shed blood unnecessarily. Surrender now and we'll let you live!"

Clouded Sky spat. "Don't pretend to be righteous, Snow Wind! I know the Emperor commissioned you to kill me!"

The Imperial Sword looked at him calmly. "I no longer have the name I once had. But you know less than you think, Clouded Sky! We did not travel all this way to find *you*." He made a gesture in the direction of the downward path, and the guards stood aside, opening up a way to freedom. "None of my men will stop you leaving. It's the girl we want."

"Come and get me!" Iron Maiden shouted, stamping her foot. "I'm not afraid!"

So they would let him leave? Clouded Sky didn't believe it for an instant. The Emperor would never subdue Hubei without crushing every single one of the Roaring Tiger rebels!

He should never have risked the greater good by coming here to fight Iron Maiden. But maybe he could still find a way to leave the fight. Without relaxing his stance, he said,

"Miss Iron, give me my spear!"

Iron Maiden did not move.

"Fine, I'll give it back. But first you should ask the Imperial Sword why he came all the way from Nanjing to arrest humble self. You, hero, are Clouded Sky, last leader of the Roaring Tiger rebels! Why does he tell you to leave? Why does he prefer to harass an ignorant girl?"

"Excellent question!" Clouded Sky turned to the Imperial Sword. "Answer her."

The Imperial Sword bowed slightly.

"Miss Iron is not so ignorant as she says, hero! She comes from Ten Thousand Thorns Temple."

"Ten Thousand Thorns Temple?" Clouded Sky laughed. "That's a story for children!"

"That doesn't mean it's not real," Iron Maiden said. She threw the broken spear into the air. "Catch!"

Many things happened at once. Iron Maiden charged the guards, the force of her palms sweeping up a raging wind. Clouded Sky leaped into the air to catch the spear—but so did the Imperial Sword. In the same instant, both of them caught hold of it, the Imperial Sword by the broken haft, Clouded Sky by the steel below the blade. When Clouded Sky tried to yank it away from the Imperial Sword with a well-placed kick, his opponent blocked him.

They landed on the ground. The Imperial Sword stabbed towards Clouded Sky's *Heaven's Five Meetings* acupoint, but he blocked the blow with his sword. Their internal forces met, slamming the combatants back, and the Imperial Sword lost his grip on the spear.

At once, Clouded Sky reversed his grip. Now he had two weapons. He turned, looking for the path down the mountain, but found that Iron Maiden at his back fighting off what seemed like all the guards at once.

"Stay with me, hero!" she called to him. "Watch my back!"

Then she attacked, palms and fists and feet flying. She feinted left and attacked right; her feet struck north and south at once. With each stroke, she felled a man. Sabres and spears hummed around her head, but she paid no attention to her back. The Imperial Sword dashed in and aimed a piercing flurry of strokes at her acupoints, but Clouded Sky met him with his sword.

In the chaos of the fight, he thought she spared him a smile.

Then they burst through the encirclement and could unleash their lightness skill. Their flight brought them down the jagged cliffs and tumbled stone of the mountain in a swift, plummeting series of leaps and bounds.

Clouded Sky's horse was tethered among the bamboo at the foot of the mountain. Clouded Sky reached him first, and rather than untie the halter he sliced it with his sword as he vaulted into the saddle. A moment later Iron Maiden settled as lightly as a bird behind him. Two more flying daggers hissed down from the heights of the mountain and buried themselves in the bamboo stems beside them. Clouded Sky snatched one of them as the horse sprang into motion.

Just in time. Spears rained down behind them with a racket of splitting and singing bamboo.

As the white horse sped into a gallop, Iron Maiden laughed. "They won't catch us now. What a beautiful horse! What's his name?"

"Flying Crane."

"Flying Crane," she repeated in delight. She said the name in a way that made the horse, in some indefinable way, hers.

Once they had left the mountain a safe distance behind them, Clouded Sky slowed the horse to a trot.

"We shouldn't be together, Miss Iron. When we're safe, you should leave."

She laughed again. "Hero has decided not to kill me, then?"

He ignored the comment. "The Imperial Sword is dangerous. Do you see these?" He held up the flying dagger so she could see it over his shoulder. "Venomous Knives. They are used by a renegade martial artist named Snow Wind."

"Snow Wind," Iron Maiden repeated thoughtfully. "I don't think I've exchanged stances with anyone going by that name."

"He uses the name Imperial Sword now. He's danger-ous. Even if I could handle him, I can't fight forty imperial guards on my own. If we split up, the Imperial Sword will be forced to divide his men and hunt both of us."

"If we split up, he'll look for me. He said he was willing

23

to let you go."

"The word of an evil one means nothing at all!" Clouded Sky gritted his teeth. "I'm a rebel, and now the self-styled Emperor has to kill me to prove the righteousness of his authority. He must execute me just as he executed my foster-father Roaring Tiger and my blood-brother Broken Spear. Not only that, but I'm the only one left who might be able to unite the Mount Jing troops and force the Emperor's Red Turbans to leave Hubei. Believe me, they will come for me."

Iron Maiden was silent for a moment. "Clouded Sky *dage*, I'm sorry."

Dage. Elder brother. Now *he* belonged to her.

She tapped the wooden box across his shoulders. "So, the spear belonged to your blood-brother?"

He nodded. "I'm taking it back to our master at Wudang Mountain. It was his last wish."

"How did the Emperor capture them?"

He'd fled all the way from Nanjing hiding his face, not daring to speak to anyone, grieving the loss of his dearest friends in the world. What did it say for the injustice in this world that this renegade girl was the only person he could trust? Clouded Sky sighed.

"We were in correspondence with a number of officials at the Emperor's court. Upon certain concessions from Duke Roaring Tiger, they would convince the Emperor to withdraw his troops from our territory. Roaring Tiger believed they were sincere, but they insisted on

24

a personal meeting. So we went to Nanjing in disguise."
He struggled to suppress his emotion as he remembered
what happened next. "When Roaring Tiger and Broken
Spear went to see the officials, they were met by imperial
guards.

"As luck would have it, I didn't go to the meeting. I fell
ill and had to remain at our lodgings. By the time I found
out what was happening, Roaring Tiger and Broken Spear
had both been executed for treason.

"I should have listened to Broken Spear. Before he left
he told me he was afraid something was going to happen.
He made me promise that if anything happened to him, I
would return his spear to Wudang Mountain."

"The Vastly Martial Emperor must be stopped," Iron
Maiden said softly.

"How?" Clouded Sky sighed. "Some would say he has
the Mandate of Heaven. Maybe it's true. It would explain
why none can resist him."

Iron Maiden snorted. "With that attitude, Elder will
certainly fail! To stop a man like the Emperor one must
have a vanquish-dragons-and-subdue-tigers ability, a
contain-the-river-and-embrace-the-ocean vision! How
can a robber and murderer like the Vastly Martial Emperor have the Mandate of Heaven?"

"Miss Iron, how can humble self judge the Emperor's
actions to be right or wrong? I prefer to accept what is and
work for the greater good." Clouded Sky spoke politely
but through gritted teeth. Iron Maiden was nothing but a

peasant bandit, making ignorant and foolish judgements. Here was All-Under-Heaven in war and chaos, and all she cared about was terrorising people and trying to prove herself supreme in martial arts!

"The night before he died," Clouded Sky continued, "Broken Spear told me of the vision in his heart. A world without chaos, without massacres and wars. A world where all life is precious and loved, even little birds in their nests. A world where we might live at peace in our homes, tilling the earth, instead of fighting for our survival…" He cleared his throat. "Miss Iron, maybe it is small, but I would prefer to spend my life fighting to make Broken Spear's vision come true. Not trying to prove myself supreme in the martial arts world."

"Humility is not the same thing as smallness, *dage*. The real question is, do you believe it can come true? And are you willing to do whatever necessary to bring it about?"

Clouded Sky bowed his head. "I must. It's not just my own vision. It's Broken Spear's, too."

Flying Crane jogged on steadily for a few paces before Iron Maiden spoke again.

"There is a way to achieve this vision, *dage*. And I know how it can be done. In seeking to exchange stances with martial artists, I am not trying to prove my supremacy. I am looking for a worthy ally. Ever since I left Ten Thousand Thorns Temple, I have been searching the whole martial arts world for someone with the kind of vision and ability that we need. Please, let me tell you the

26

whole story."

* * *

Hero knows that one hundred years ago, the last Song Emperors struggled to rule a divided world. Those were the days of the great Yuan invasion from beyond the Wall. With their horse-mounted armies, they pierced through the Wall and began to conquer All-Under-Heaven. The first to fall were the kingdoms of Jin and Xia. Finally, the last Song army was defeated at the Battle of Yamen. Seeing the defeat, General Lu Xiufu took the boy Emperor in his arms and hurled himself into the sea. The leader of the conquering Yuans proclaimed himself Emperor, the Lord of a Thousand Years, the first man in five hundred years to rule *all* Under-Heaven.

Or nearly all.

On the borders of his new empire, Emperor Father-of-the-World still had to face the resistance of many brave leaders who would not accept the foreigner's yoke. They too had the dream of Broken Spear. In a tiny village in the mountains of Sichuan province, lived the Coiling Dragon King.

"That was his bandit title," said Clouded Sky, as she paused. "He wasn't a real king."

"Whether a man is a king or a bandit depends on whether you ask the Emperor or the peasants, dage. *Maybe the Emperor himself is only a very great bandit, preying on the*

27

people."

The Coiling Dragon King and his followers were famous heroes of the martial arts world, and with his Golden Phoenix Sword, the Coiling Dragon King was invincible. No matter how many armies Father-of-the-World sent against him, the Coiling Dragon King and his followers maintained their freedom, bastioned by the hills.

"Don't forget where he learned his martial arts, Miss Iron."

"Dage must be aware that he learned them from Wudang Sect. It is not commonly known, but his shifu was none other than Sect Founder Zhang."

"When I heard the story at Wudang it was different."

"Or perhaps Wudang does not remember the full story."

The Coiling Dragon King and his men protected their village and roamed the martial arts world doing justice, feeding peasants, and battling the foreign Yuan regime. He had only one misfortune to keep him awake at night: the Coiling Dragon King had no child.

The King and his wife sent up many prayers to every deity in Heaven, but none were able to help. "Maybe try the Flowers God," one would say. "Have you spoken to the Moon Rabbit? What about Numi?" They worked their way through the whole heavenly bureaucracy, until only the First Deity remained.

"He is far away and perhaps he will not hear," said Coiling Dragon King's wife. Her name was Lovely Flower.

28

"What have we got to lose, anyway?" said Coiling Dragon King. So they made their prayers, and to their delight, Lovely Flower soon began to show signs of pregnancy.

I suppose they must have made all the usual sacrifices, including the ones asking for a boy. Indeed, the baby was born healthy and beautiful...but it was not a boy. It was a girl, and they named her Morning Light.

One year after Princess Morning Light was born, Coiling Dragon King organised a great celebration for the child's First Grab ceremony. He spared no expense and invited everybody. All the heroes of the martial arts world, and even many of the gods. In the end, only the Eight Immortals came to represent Heaven. They could never resist the prospect of a party.

"That's also different to the story I heard. Only seven of the Eight Immortals came."

"Elder is quite correct. Seven of the Eight Immortals came...at first."

Before the meal of longevity noodles came the First Grab ceremony. All the guests gathered to watch. At the last minute, Coiling Dragon King unhooked the Golden Phoenix Sword from his belt and added it to the collection of symbolic items on the table. Morning Light was brought in and placed on the ground before the table to choose the occupation of her future life. She didn't even look at the books, coins, pens, and other items on the table. Instead, the little princess toddled forward

29

and grabbed the yellow tassel on the hilt of the Golden Phoenix sword.

The guests applauded, but Lovely Flower sighed.

"A warrior!" cried Coiling Dragon King with great satisfaction. "My daughter will be a martial heroine, like her father!"

Next, Coiling Dragon King asked the Eight-But-One Immortals to bestow their blessings upon the child. When they had poured enough cold water over Visiting-Caves Lu to sober him up, the Immortals gathered around where Morning Light sat happily playing with the Golden Phoenix Sword, and each of them bestowed a blessing.

"No man shall ever be led astray by her beauty," said Peaceful-Countenance Lan.

"An excess of learning will never make her arrogant," said Imperial Brother-in-Law Cao.

"She will always trust the wisdom of others above her own understanding," said Iron Crutch Li.

"Her words will always be gentle and reverent," said Hunan's-Son Han.

"She will never make enemies," said Zhongli of Han.

"Others may concern themselves for the physical nourishment of the poor," said Visiting-Caves Lu, "but she will devote herself to their spiritual enlightenment."

"And," said Old Zhang Guo, beaming in delight, "on her sixteenth birthday, after sustaining a slight injury from the Golden Phoenix Sword, she will enter into a profound meditation, through which she shall attain complete enlightenment, and from thence leave her body and ascend spiritually into Heaven."

Lovely Flower gasped in delight. A murmur of surprise and even envy arose in the hall. Only the Coiling Dragon King yanked worriedly at his beard and muttered, "Never make enemies? Ascend into Heaven? What use is a daughter like that to anyone?"

It was then that the doors of the hall flew open, and the Eighth Immortal, Lady He, flew in astride a celestial crane.

When Coiling Dragon King had recovered from his surprise at her unexpected arrival, he cupped his fists and bowed. "Immortal Lady He! Welcome to the First Grab celebration of the Princess Morning Light. Please, join us to eat Longevity Noodles!"

If he had not been so put out of countenance by the unwelcome gifts of the seven other immortals, Coiling Dragon King would have remembered that Immortal Lady He was profoundly enlightened and had long ceased to take any earthly nourishment at all.

"No, thank you, your highness," she snapped. "This penniless one would not have come, but the Flowers God sent me this memorandum and then went on a journey before I could return it." She unfolded a scrap of white silk, written in red ink.

"By the Jade Emperor's command—no, I beg your pardon. The Jade Emperor is acting on orders from higher up." She cleared her throat and raised her voice.

31

"Indeed, the Princess Morning Light shall sustain a slight injury from the Golden Phoenix Sword, and shall enter into a profound meditation, which shall continue for a hundred years. At the end of that time, an unfortunate inability to detach herself from earthly illusion will bring an end to all the blessings bestowed on her today, causing her to leave her meditation for a life of passion and struggle in the martial arts world."

A shocked silence fell upon the hall. Only Coiling Dragon King looked hopeful.

Immortal Lady He tucked the scrap of silk into her sleeve again, and bowed to Coiling Dragon King. "Your highness, please accept my sympathy in your misfortune. I'm acting on the *highest* orders."

With that, she climbed onto her celestial crane again and left.

From that time on, Coiling Dragon King kept the Golden Phoenix Sword locked deep within five chests, where he could be sure that Morning Light would never touch it. Indeed, he forbade his followers even to mention the name of the sword.

"Doesn't Virtuous Husband *want* her to attain enlightenment?" Lovely Flower protested.

"Of course I do," said Coiling Dragon King. "Maybe when she's sixty!"

But the decrees of Heaven can never be thwarted. Princess Morning Light grew, and her temperament was not just warm and charming; it was also bold and fearless.

By the time she was twelve years old, Morning Light had already mastered all the stances that Coiling Dragon King could teach her. He began to consider sending her to Wudang Mountain to learn from his martial brothers there, but before he could do so, a crisis arose.

In the Year of the Monkey, Emperor Father-of-the-World sent an army to subdue the mountains, and Coiling Dragon King marched away to meet them. Most of his men never returned. After many months, Coiling Dragon King's lieutenant Wild Goose returned home. His clothes were in rags and his shoes were in tatters, but he carried the Golden Phoenix Sword safely on his back.

According to Coiling Dragon King's last wishes, Morning Light and Wild Goose would marry, and together they would defend their village from the Yuan Emperor. Lovely Flower was crushed by her husband's death, but she had not forgotten the prophecy made by Old Zhang Guo at Morning Light's First Grab celebration. Secretly, she waited, hoped, and prayed for the day when her beloved daughter would be freed from the sorrows and misfortunes of earthly attachments. Whenever Wild Goose asked Lovely Flower to be his matchmaker with Morning Light, Lovely Flower put him off with the excuse that Morning Light still needed to finish her training with her martial uncles at Wudang Mountain.

On Morning Light's sixteenth birthday, Lovely Flower stole to the shrine to her late husband's shrine, unlocked each of the five chests, and presented Morning Light with

33

the Golden Phoenix Sword.

Morning Light had never dreamed that such a beautiful thing existed. She was delighted by the blade's lightness and balance, by the golden patterns etched into the steel, by the way it rang like a bell when she struck it with her fingernail, the way it hissed and shimmered and sang when she swung it through the air. At once, she ran to the courtyard and began to move through the eighty-eight stances of Coiling Dragon King's Heaven-Relying Dragon-Slaying Sword Skill.

"The Heaven-Relying Dragon-Slaying Sword Skill!" Clouded Sky shook his head. "If anything could give a martial artist unbeatable skill, that could! But it's been lost for a hundred years."

Iron Maiden smiled.

Morning Light knew each of the stances to perfection, but she was unaccustomed to the length, the flexibility, and above all the perfect balance of the Golden Phoenix Sword. It almost had a speed and power of its own, and as Morning Light moved through the stances it flickered faster and faster. Morning Light flitted like a butterfly and roared like a tiger. She stabbed the north and pierced the south; she struck the west and lunged to the east. At last, as she executed the final stance of the Heaven-Relying Dragon-Slaying Sword Skill, the Golden Phoenix Sword struck faster than she could see. Faster than she could move.

A tiny cut appeared on her left forefinger.

34

Morning Light gave a cry that was half pain and half delight. She licked her finger and sat cross-legged on the ground. A little cultivation of her *qi* energy, and the cut would heal. But a soft voice stopped her. Lovely Flower stood under the verandah, looking down on her.

"You should go and meditate in the temple, child." As Morning Light jumped to her feet and ran off, Lovely Flower murmured, "You must not be left in the rain and the snow."

Morning Light ran into the temple and sat down before the gods. Holding the Golden Phoenix Sword across her knees, she closed her eyes and began to meditate. Immediately she fell into a deeper trance than she had ever experienced before. She realised the illusory nature of desire, attachment, and anger. She understood the ineffable truth of all things.

Revelation flooded her heart and illuminated her mind.

* * *

Clouded Sky waited for Iron Maiden to go on, but she remained silent.

"Is that the end of the story?"

Iron Maiden sighed. "It's sad, isn't it? Morning Light might have been a martial heroine to rival her father. Instead, she was stuck inside a temple, aloof from the martial arts world!"

"Morning Light experienced perfect enlightenment,

35

the goal of all martial discipline. What better is there? The story I heard says that the princess still sits there in the temple in the mountains, guarded by ten thousand thorns. It says that some of the greatest heroes of the martial arts world have gone in search of her, to retrieve the Golden Phoenix Sword and learn the secret of the Heaven-Relying Dragon-Slaying Sword Skill. None of them ever succeeded."

"None of them knew the way to Ten Thousand Thorns Temple. But I do." Clouded Sky went cold suddenly, and turned in the saddle, trying to see her face.

"Is that your plan? We go in search of Morning Light? You can't be serious!"

"Why wouldn't I be serious, *dage*? According to the prophecy of Immortal Lady He, Morning Light would wake from her meditations after a hundred years. The hundred years have now passed. We have to wake her and return the Heaven-Relying Dragon-Slaying Sword Skill, the Golden Phoenix Sword, and Coiling Dragon King's army of peerless martial artists to the martial arts world! Only then can we hope to defeat the Emperor and bring peace to All-Under-Heaven."

The Heaven-Relying Dragon-Slaying Sword Skill! Clouded Sky's skin prickled as he thought of the charlatans who roamed the martial arts world, selling what they claimed were original versions of Coiling Dragon King's long-lost sword manual. If it was really possible to recover this lost skill, his name would never be forgotten. He would truly be the supreme martial artist; neither Iron Maiden nor anyone else would be able to defeat him. He could forge an alliance between Morning Light and the Roaring Tiger rebels, and lead them against the Vastly Martial Emperor. That is, unless the Vastly Martial Emperor reached Mount Jing first and dispersed, starved or slaughtered the rebels to extinction.

"It's impossible," he said at last. "The Emperor is about to destroy the rest of the Mount Jing rebels, and you want me to run away with you on a wild goose chase?"

Iron Maiden laughed. "No, not a Wild Goose chase. The village chief is Valuable Ox now."

Clouded Sky frowned. "So you've been there yourself? Why didn't *you* wake Morning Light?"

"I tried." Iron Maiden sighed. "But you know that the temple is protected by ten thousand thorns. It would take a great hero to battle his way through them, and after that, it is only a deep attachment to the martial arts world that will succeed in waking Morning Light. Humble self is not worthy."

Despite himself, Clouded Sky was touched by her humble tone. "Your martial skill is profound, Miss Iron! Apart from my blood brother, Broken Spear, and my *shifu*, Harmonious Virtue, I doubt I've exchanged stances with a more accomplished warrior. Your skill is far above mine. If yours is insufficient, then mine certainly will be."

Iron Maiden was quiet for a moment. At last she said, "The martial skill is important, but so is the ocean-

37

embracing vision and the reliance upon Heaven. You, Clouded Sky, do you really wish to bring peace and prosperity to All-Under-Heaven?"

"Of course I do. But there are greater heroes than myself in the martial arts world. You should find one of them."

"Your martial arts are not so bad! Wudang Sect may not be what it once was, but your basic skills are strong; you only need a little improvement. I am only an ignorant girl, but there are one or two things I can teach you."

Train under Iron Maiden? He, a Wudang disciple? Clouded Sky tried not to be offended. "Taoist Priest Harmonious Virtue is my *shifu*."

"That's why you ought to train with me. So you can learn what he isn't teaching you."

He was momentarily speechless. It was unthinkable to learn martial arts from anyone without his *shifu*'s express permission—a permission which he would never seek, because it would be tantamount to accusing his *shifu* of failure.

"I can get additional instruction from Harmonious Virtue anytime."

"I thought you wanted to *defeat* the Vastly Martial Emperor!"

"You go too far, Miss Iron!"

"Do I? You couldn't defeat me, and I know next to nothing. You couldn't even protect your blood brother!"

"How dare you insult Wudang Sect!" Clouded Sky

jerked his horse to a stop, then jumped to the ground and unsheathed his sword in one motion. "Wudang Sect is the leader of the martial arts world, and I will prove it!"

Iron Maiden sniffed. "Of course it is! Everyone knows that! That doesn't change the fact that I could defeat you in one stance. How is that an insult?"

"You said my *shifu* had not taught me well enough to—to—to protect…" Clouded Sky pressed his lips together, and the hand that held his black sword began to shake.

"But he hasn't," Iron Maiden said. Her voice softened as she saw him struggle with the force of his emotions. "I didn't mean to insult your *shifu*, Elder, but it's not worth fighting about. We ought to be helping each other escape the Imperial Sword, not killing each other!"

With an effort, Clouded Sky calmed himself.

"Sometimes it is necessary to turn one's back on smaller matters in order to serve the greater good, but if you disrespect my sect or *shifu* again, I'll have to kill you!"

"Much appreciated, hero!"

"And my martial arts is as good as it needs to be!"

"Prove it, then." Iron Maiden slid off the horse and assumed a stance, her eyes sparkling with fun. "No challenge. Just a friendly exchange of stances."

She needed to learn a lesson. Willing to oblige, Clouded Sky attacked with the stance *Piercing the Pearl*, stabbing toward Iron Maiden's forehead. His attack was lightning-fast, but she countered, shifting her head to the side even as her fingers shot out, aiming for an acupoint. Clouded Sky had expected the move, and his sword had already changed direction. But it was only a feint: while his attention was on her hands, she kicked an acupoint in his leg. He collapsed with a groan of pain.

Iron Maiden retreated, and began to stroke Flying Crane's nose.

Clouded Sky circulated his *qi* to open the acupoint, buying time to think. He had lost. Again. She must have deliberately provoked his anger to get the upper hand more easily.

He calmed his mind and tried to cultivate an attitude of detachment as he climbed to his feet and adopted another stance.

"Again?" Iron Maiden shook her head with a sigh. As Clouded Sky charged, she unleashed a palm-strike in his direction, so powerful that it created gales of wind as she swept toward him. If he had not met the stroke with his sword, it would have broken bones. As it was, it threw him off his feet. Iron Maiden soared lightly through the air after him.

As he leaped from to his feet, she met him with a jab to the *Great Welcome* acupoint.

Clouded Sky went down. Iron Maiden bent over him.

"Your sword is extraordinarily powerful," she said thoughtfully. "You must practice with it constantly. If you only let it tell you what to do, you would almost not need my teaching." She tapped his acupoint thrice, releasing him, and then helped him climb to his feet.

He was exhausted from all the fighting, and his body ached from Iron Maiden's punishment. Clouded Sky hesitated before wearily sheathing his sword.

"I admit it, Miss Iron. You are better than me."

She smiled. "So you will come with me to Ten Thousand Thorns Temple?"

"No. Princess Morning Light has achieved enlightenment and is free of this unhappy world. To draw her back would be an unrighteous act!"

Iron Maiden was incredulous. "Unrighteous? But it's the duty of every righteous warrior to punish injustice! The self-styled emperor uproots and slays innocent people, filling their lives with misery—how can it be unrighteous to help them?"

"I will help them. Just not like this. If Morning Light is destined to wake, she will do so whether I interfere or not."

"A person who is in such a deep meditation will not awake without some significant assistance, hero. You heard the story. The will of Heaven must be carried out!"

"But not by me. As I told you, I must return to Mount Jing."

There was a short and disappointed silence. "*Dage*, if you are going to Mount Jing to take charge of the rebels, then you are doing a righteous thing. I can't object to that. But don't go and fight the Emperor with such an important part of your training missing!"

41

Clouded Sky hesitated. He could no longer ignore the fact that Iron Maiden was right. His martial arts were lacking. But to learn from a renegade wanderer? Just asking for permission to do such a thing would cause Harmonious Virtue to lose face.

"A day or two and you'll know everything I can teach you!" Iron Maiden looked hopeful.

"You're right," he said gently. "I do need more training. Don't worry. Before I return to Mount Jing, I'll ask Harmonious Virtue if he will consent to train me further."

And it would be orthodox training, too. Not Iron Maiden's dangerous heresies.

She looked so crestfallen that he was afraid she was going to cry.

"Good luck in your search, Miss Iron," he said hurriedly, and vaulted onto Flying Crane's back. As Clouded Sky cantered away, he imagined the dejection on her face as she watched him go. What other choice did he have?

Chapter 2.

For the sake of secrecy, the Imperial Sword's men kept perfect silence as they marched. Overhead the bright moon hovered like a golden pearl above the horizon, shedding a pale light in the dark valley where he and his men travelled. Allusive half-sentences about the moon, the valley, and the goal that he pursued melded together in the Imperial Sword's mind, creating a vast web of intricate meaning and double meaning. When he had the chance, he would write them down. If they were as good as he thought, he might have a poem.

Footsteps pattered along the river toward them. Imperial Sword thumbed his sword loose in the sheath, but when the figure emerged from the dusk, it proved to be Second Brother. The bounty hunter had vanished during the fight on the mountain, and Imperial Sword had put him out of mind. Imperial Sword was careful not to reveal his surprise.

"You again," he said. "Do you have more information for me?"

The bounty hunter bowed profoundly.

"I have good news and bad news, your excellency. I tracked Clouded Sky's horse all the way to Peony Settlement. He must have arrived an hour ago."

"And the Iron Maiden?"

Second Brother shook his head. "She left him at some point along the way. I would tell your excellency where, but she must have employed her lightness skill in leaving. There were no tracks on the ground."

The Imperial Sword schooled his face to show none of the exasperation he felt. After the fight at the temple he had lost valuable time getting his wounded men down the mountain. By the time he was ready to continue the chase, Clouded Sky and Iron Maiden were long out of sight, and unlike Second Brother, his men weren't good enough trackers to follow a horse's trail through the forest.

He'd had to assume that Iron Maiden would recruit Clouded Sky to travel west with her to Ten Thousand Thorns Temple, and even if she didn't, Clouded Sky was headed west past Wudang anyway. So in the end, he'd decided to cut across country in hope of picking them up on the west road. He'd known it was risky if the pair of them split up, but he'd gambled on Clouded Sky being eager to recover the Heaven-Relying Dragon-Slaying Sword Skill. Gambled, and lost.

"Is Clouded Sky still in the settlement?"

"Yes, your excellency. The old woman I spoke to said he had gone to the inn. I checked the stable. There was a white horse."

The Imperial Sword nodded. "We'll have to question him. If Iron Maiden has shared her secrets with him, he might be useful to us. If not, he's the only one who can tell us where she was last seen."

Second Brother smiled and stroked his weapons.

The Imperial Sword grabbed his wrist. "No wanton killing! Do you hear me? I want Clouded Sky alive and talking. Otherwise..." He swallowed. Maybe the Emperor was right. Maybe a clean kill today was better than a rebellion tomorrow. "Otherwise, kill anyone who resists."

* * *

The window of Clouded Sky's room faced west. If he leaned out, he could just see the purple shoulders of Wudang Mountain fading into the darkening southern sky. The Taoist monastery on its high ridge was just two days' journey from Peony Settlement, and somewhere in the darkness beyond was Mount Jing and the Roaring Tiger rebels. Once he reached Wudang, he would have to send word that he was alive and returning to them.

This late in the evening, only a few people went to and fro in the street, hurrying to their homes before night closed in. A figure in a reed hat came along the street from the east, and as it passed the window, the hat tilted back to reveal a pale smudge of face peering up at him. Hurriedly, Clouded Sky drew back and closed the window. Here in

Peony Settlement there were no wanted posters staring at him with his own eyes, but all the same he needed to avoid drawing attention to himself. It could not be too much longer before the Emperor marched into Hubei to smash the Mount Jing troops once and for all. Some would jump at the chance to win the Emperor's favour by delivering Clouded Sky to him as an appetiser.

The room was a good one and the bed looked inviting. In the days when Clouded Sky and Broken Spear had roamed the martial arts world, fighting injustice and helping the needy, they had often stayed in taverns much worse than this one, each taking turns to watch while the other slept. Now Broken Spear was dead and once more he was forced to doze or meditate upright in a corner, his sword ready in his hands.

Exhausted as he was, Clouded Sky dreaded the nights. In the dark it was easy to imagine the ghosts of his foster father and blood brother rising up to reproach him. There ought to have been something he could have done. He should have been able to save them...

Clouded Sky rearranged the covers on the bed to make it appear as though a body was lying there, and then seated himself in a dark corner with a good view of both the window and the door. He settled his sword across his knees and tried to meditate, but ever since Broken Spear's death, calm had evaded him.

Was there any truth in Iron Maiden's story? Where had she learned her martial arts? Even if Princess Morning

Light was real, and even if she could be woken from her meditation, why would she agree to help him? What if she chose to support the Emperor instead?

Better not to consider it. He had to go to Wudang first and then Mount Jing.

Even if Morning Light was willing to lead her followers to defend Hubei, the Vastly Martial Emperor still claimed the Mandate of Heaven. And not without reason. He commanded thousands of troops. In the wake of the Yuans' downfall, he had extended his power over most of All-Under-Heaven. With the stroke of a brush he had condemned Broken Spear and Roaring Tiger to death, and now Clouded Sky himself was a fugitive in his own province. If Heaven and Earth sanctioned the Vastly Martial Emperor's mandate, surely it was foolish to dream of something better.

Movement outside the window startled him from his thoughts. Clouded Sky drew his sword and rose to his feet. Some iron implement slithered through the gap between the two shutters and lifted the latch. The hinges murmured as the shutters opened. Then a dark shadow flitted across the square of pale sky beyond, and feet landed softly on the floorboards.

Clouded Sky extended his sword like a bar before the intruder's chest. Hidden in the deep shadows, his eyes were better adjusted to the darkness inside the room. He was not surprised to see that the intruder wore a reed hat slipped off the head onto the shoulders.

47

"Miss Iron, why are you following me?"

"*Dage*! You need my help," Iron Maiden whispered. "The Imperial Sword saw us together today and now he is here to find you."

"Here? In Peony Settlement?"

"Coming up the street."

Clouded Sky moved to the open window and peered out, careful not to show himself to watchers below. A thin line of guards, their sabres gleaming in the fitful moonlight, quietly surrounded the tavern.

"Did they see you?"

"No, *dage*."

Clouded Sky rubbed his tired eyes. "We'll have to fight them."

"Or we could run away. Where's your horse?"

"Unsaddled in the stable." It was too late to saddle up now. And without Flying Crane, he didn't have a hope of evading the imperial guards. "Do you have a horse, Miss Iron? How did you get here so quickly?"

"I used my lightness skill."

She seemed to have inexhaustible reserves of *qi* energy at her disposal. He could well imagine her fleeting tirelessly through the treetops in swift, graceful bounds. But after today's exertions, his own *qi* was drained. He'd be lucky to jump from the window to the ground without breaking bones.

He shook his head. "We need another option."

There was a moment's silence. Then, faintly, within

48

the tavern, they heard a soft *creak*.

"They're coming," Iron Maiden said. "We'll have to get rid of them some other way. Quickly, hero! Get into bed."

"Into *bed?*"

"Yes. Quick! Let your hair down. Give me your sword." Her hands fluttered at him insistently.

Clouded Sky backed away. "Leave me alone! Are you completely shameless?"

"Don't yell, *dage*. We have to make you look harmless. It's a strategem. I don't remember where I heard it, but—"

Halfway through an indrawn breath, Clouded Sky understood.

"You mean—*Zhuge Liang Playing the Lute.*"

"Is that what it's called?"

"Or *The Empty Fort.* Thirty-Second Stratagem." He threw her his sword, undid the cord holding his hair in its topknot, and yanked off his coat and boots, leaving them scattered across the floor. Iron Maiden laid the sword next to them. Clouded Sky pointed to the door. "Unlatch it."

He rolled into the bed and pulled the blankets over his shoulders. Iron Maiden flitted soundlessly across the room and set the door ajar. Then she melted into the shadows in the corner behind it.

Clouded Sky half closed his eyes and lay breathing slowly and heavily, counting his heartbeat. His eyes moved ceaselessly from the dim patch of sky beyond the open window, to the dark outline of the cracked door.

Beyond the door, clothing rustled and blades whispered. Clouded Sky forced himself to go on breathing. In the hush of night, he heard everything with unbearable clarity. There was a soft fumbling at the latch, and Clouded Sky thought the door swung open a little further.

There was silence.

* * *

On the other side of the door, the intruders paused to consider. The door was open. Why was the door open? A man like Clouded Sky did not leave doors open.

Standing behind the door, Iron Maiden smiled.

The imperial guards worked up their courage and pushed the door further open. Iron Maiden shifted her weight a little, raising her palms.

Outside the room, the imperial guards whispered nervously. Not just the door stood open; the window was open too. Clouded Sky lay in bed sleeping, his sword halfway across the room. A man like Clouded Sky simply did not leave himself open to attack like this. There must be more to the situation than met the eye. Maybe Clouded Sky was drunk.

Or maybe he was the bait in some awful trap.

* * *

From his bed, Clouded Sky imagined he saw the glitter

of eyes at the open door.

For a moment, the moon found an opening in the dark clouds overhead and the light in the room grew stronger. Pale beams reached through the window and glimmered off the black hilt of Clouded Sky's sword, lying far out of his reach.

He stared at it longingly. Maybe he ought to have thought twice before agreeing to this plan.

The door opened a little further. This time, the hinges groaned. There was a tense silence. Clouded Sky gave up trying to breathe evenly. If they charged, would he make it to his sword in time? Or would he die half-dressed and barefoot like a beggar? Not the way he would have chosen. The silence stretched out. He wished they would just attack. Then the worst happened.

Iron Maiden laughed.

In one leap, Clouded Sky sprang from the bed, all his being focused on the sword-hilt. Ages seemed to pass before he reached it. But as he tore it from the sheath and faced the open door with his heart pounding like a hammer, he saw that the mass of bodies outside the door was gone. Instead, panicked footsteps and hurried curses jostled down the stairs.

"Ambush! Ambush! Run!"

Beside the door, Iron Maiden slid down the wall and crumpled to the floor, giving her laughter free rein. Elsewhere in the tavern, doors creaked and shutters banged as other guests tried to figure out what was going

51

on.

"Fire!" some yelled.

"Thieves!" said others.

Clouded Sky ran to the window and looked out. Below, men boiled out of the tavern door. Conspicuous in his mask, the Imperial Sword tried to hold them back.

But his efforts were futile. Iron Maiden rushed across the room and leaned out of the window with her long hair floating free in the wind.

"Flee!" she screeched. "The Demoness with the Painted Skin has come to eat your hearts!"

At the sight of this uncanny apparition, the Imperial guards yelled in terror and rushed down the street. Spitting curses beneath his mask, the Imperial Sword was forced to follow them.

As the guards faded into the distance, Iron Maiden dissolved into laughter once again. Clouded Sky put a hand to his galloping heart and sat down on the bed again, shaking and sweating. "You really ought to restrain your rejoicing, Miss Iron! If their minds had been less clouded by fear, they would have known it was a strategem."

She turned away from the window with a smile. "But, *dage,* we have learned something, haven't we? They are more afraid of us than we are of them!"

"Perhaps it would be wise to be afraid of them, Miss Iron."

"Perhaps it would be wisest of all to act righteously and rely on Heaven, *dage!*" Iron Maiden closed the shutters.

"We should be safe here tonight. You ought to sleep, Elder. I'll watch. We have a long journey tomorrow."

Clouded Sky blinked. "*We* have a long journey? May I ask what you mean by that, Miss Iron?"

"Oh! I'm coming with you to Wudang Mountain."

"You're coming with me to *where?*"

"Don't be so shocked! I've always wanted to see Wudang Mountain! Besides, they say Wudang Sect is unparalleled in the martial arts world. If you don't want to make the journey to Ten Thousand Thorns Temple, then maybe one of your martial brothers will be interested!" She paused. "Besides, it's my fault the Imperial Sword is hunting you. Since we fought them together, they think I might have recruited you. If we travel to Wudang together, we've got a better chance of getting there alive."

Clouded Sky imagined what his sect elders might think of Iron Maiden, or worse still, what Iron Maiden might think and then *say*, about his sect elders. Worst of all, there seemed no respectful way to refuse her. "I can't prevent you from travelling to Wudang, Miss Iron. But you ought to be more careful. Not everyone at Wudang will be as understanding as I am. If my martial brothers heard some of the things you've said to me, you might soon find yourself fighting the whole sect!"

"All right, hero! I'll be respectful."

Clouded Sky felt no happier. "Who are you, anyway, Miss Iron? Who was your *shifu?* What's your real name?"

"They call me Iron Maiden. I don't remember anything

else."

It was too dark to see her face, but he knew she was waiting hopefully for him to agree to her request. Clouded Sky inwardly groaned. If she wouldn't even tell him her real name or the name of her *shifu*, how could he trust her?

But she had saved his life.

Indeed, she might have been halfway to Wudang by now. She didn't need to come to Peony Settlement to warn him about the Imperial Sword. Maybe he owed her something after all.

Besides, if he took her to Wudang, he would be helping her without actually having to *help* her. Clouded Sky relented.

"You saved my life, heroine. Thank you. I'll be happy to take you to Wudang."

Heroine. Even in the dark, he sensed her smile.

"Wake me after three hours," he directed, sheathing his sword and rolling into the bed. "Then I'll watch and you can sleep. We'll leave for Wudang at dawn."

* * *

It was undignified and unbecoming for a man of Imperial Sword's stature to give way to anger. Standing before his shamefaced troops in a forest clearing outside Peony Settlement, at first he merely allowed them time to perceive the stiff outrage in his bearing. They were deep in unsubdued Hubei. No allies. No reinforcements. This far from Nanjing, cowardice could be deadly. At last he spoke in a voice full of soft menace.

"Which part of my orders did you fail to understand? Once you entered by the door, Second Brother and I would enter by the window. Clouded Sky was the only one there. You faced worse danger outside the temple this morning. What do you have to say for yourselves?"

A chorus of voices answered him.

"It was an ambush!"

"There was a demon hiding behind the door!"

"The whole village knew we were coming!"

"A demon," said Imperial Sword. "Is that what you think?"

"It laughed at us. Horrible!"

"Superstitious idiots, fleeing while no one pursued." Second Brother drew two sharp hooks from his back. "It was the girl, of course. We should kill them all, your excellency. You and I alone would do a better job than these cowards!"

His men dared not speak, but they looked at him pleadingly. Kill them all? Startled out of his self-command, the Imperial Sword tightened his fists.

"No!"

"They're deserters! Worthless! The Vastly Martial Emperor would have them torn apart by wild horses."

Almost before Imperial Sword knew what he was doing, he swept his sword out of the sheath and pointed it at

Second Brother. "Worthless peasant! *I* represent the Emperor here, not you."

To his astonishment, rather than cringe in fear, the bounty hunter smiled. For an instant Imperial Sword thought he read a challenge in Second Brother's face. Then, still smiling, he lowered his hooks and bowed. "Your excellency, forgive the excessive devotion of the Emperor's loyal servant."

Second Brother's words were humble but Imperial Sword perceived their true meaning, and it chilled his heart. He knew the Emperor did not yet fully trust him. He knew this mission was intended to prove his loyalty, and that one false step would cost him his life.

He knew that if he made that false step, Second Brother would be ready and willing to inform the Emperor for the sake of his own personal advancement. He didn't owe the man an explanation, but he thought it wise to make one anyway.

"We're miles away from Nanjing in rebellious territory. If Clouded Sky and Iron Maiden have joined forces again, we're going to need all the men we can get."

Without a word, Second Brother bowed again.

"But your devotion to the Emperor is commendable!" The Imperial Sword turned toward his men. "The next time you worthless ones show such cowardice, I won't restrain him!"

At once, the guards kowtowed, murmuring their gratitude. The Imperial Sword gave orders to make camp. As the men dispersed to unsaddle their horses, he beckoned Second Brother closer.

"You speak like a man who fears nothing at all, Second Brother. Perhaps you think your martial skill is equal to mine."

"Perhaps I think it is better, your excellency."

A malicious aura flickered around Second Brother. But the martial arts world was full of haughty and arrogant warriors. Under his mask, the Imperial Sword smiled.

"You don't know who I really am, do you?"

Second Brother looked at him blankly.

"Truly it is said that there is no wisdom like silence," Imperial Sword observed. "Meditate on that, Second Brother."

* * *

Clouded Sky and Iron Maiden arrived at Wudang on the second evening of their journey from Peony Settlement. They did not see the guards again during their flight, but Clouded Sky knew the Imperial Sword couldn't be far away.

"Look." They stood high on the long stair that led up the mountainside to the monastery perched above. Before them was a heaving countryside of forests, rivers and hills, overlaid with a haze of blue mist. Clouded Sky pointed north several *li* to where a flock of white birds had risen into the sky and now circled above their roost.

"The Emperor's men are still following us." Iron Maiden frowned. "I thought that when we turned toward Wudang they would give up, or perhaps wait to ambush us when we leave. They're too close."

The birds drifted on the air, sometimes seeming to melt into the clouds as their white feathers reflected the blue evening light.

"*Dage*, is it safe here?"

"Safe?" Clouded Sky shook his head. "This is Wudang Mountain, heroine. If we aren't safe here, then no place under Heaven is."

They found the monastery perched high on the mountain's slope, a cluster of tiled roofs, red walls, and grey cobbled courtyards linked by sudden stairs. There was a cold bite in the air; by morning, there would be a frost.

The monastery's heavy gate was still open, and the old gatekeeper called Clouded Sky by name as they went through into the courtyard beyond.

"Martial cousin! You've returned!" He turned on his stool and lifted his voice. "Clouded Sky is here! Clouded Sky is still alive!"

As he cupped his fists, Clouded Sky couldn't help smiling just as broadly as the gatekeeper.

"Elder, where is *shifu*?"

"At this time, he ought to be in the temple courtyard."

Clouded Sky bowed again and led the way toward the temple. There were an unusual number of people about. In addition to the Taoist priests that lived at the monastery, travellers and beggars gossiped or dozed under the verandahs. Clouded Sky guessed that they must have fled from the Emperor's wars.

The gatekeeper's call brought disciples running into the courtyard. Soon Clouded Sky was surrounded by a crowd of his martial brothers and cousins.

"It's Clouded Sky! Where have you been? How did you survive?

"Who is this lovely maiden? What is she doing with an ugly fellow like you?"

Before he could answer, Iron Maiden called out.

"I'm Iron Maiden, and I'm his bodyguard. Make way!" She aimed a palm at the nearest disciple, and sent him flying through the crowd. Laughing disciples scattered to left and right, clearing the path ahead of them.

"*Shifu* first, disciples later," she said.

"You deserve it for calling me ugly, martial brother," Clouded Sky added, stepping over the disciple lying on the ground. But as they left the martial brothers and cousins behind them, he murmured, "Please let me do the talking from now on, heroine."

"Whatever you like, *dage*."

"And the fighting. Especially the fighting."

She gave a disappointed sigh, but didn't argue with him. They soon reached the temple courtyard, where a class of young disciples no more than nine and ten years of age practised their basic stances under the watchful eye of a sect elder.

"Taoist Priest Harmonious Virtue!" Clouded Sky dropped the small bundle of personal belongings he'd been carrying since they left Flying Crane at the mountain's foot. "*Shifu!*"

The old priest looked up and his mouth opened in delighted astonishment.

"Clouded Sky! Disciple!" A little shaky with age, he circled the young disciples and came down to meet them. "Truly, one happiness scatters a thousand sorrows. They told me you were dead!"

Clouded Sky bowed deeply.

"*Shifu*, the truth is not much better. Humble self has escaped, but I was the only one. Roaring Tiger and Broken Spear were both beheaded." He held out the wooden box which he had carried so far. "Broken Spear asked me to bring you this."

Harmonious Virtue took the box with trembling hands and slid open the lid. His long white moustache quivered.

"Broken Spear was my finest pupil, his martial skill matched only by his understanding. Ah! War is Death's feast. But you, Clouded Sky, how did you escape?"

Clouded Sky glanced at the little disciples still practising their stances. Harmonious Virtue followed his glance.

"Yes, let us speak privately." He closed the box and motioned for Clouded Sky and Iron Maiden to follow him beyond the temple to a quiet courtyard which overlooked the south hills toward Mount Jing.

"There are Imperial guards on our trail." Clouded Sky

dropped his voice. "We know they are less than six *li* from here and still travelling."

The old priest stroked his beard.

"Are they coming here?"

"I'm afraid they might. They have a powerful martial artist with them; he uses venomous knives."

"Snow Wind?"

"I believe so."

Harmonious Virtue looked thoughtful.

"Snow Wind is listed as the fourth greatest warrior in the martial arts world."

"I fear he and his men may be planning to attack."

Clouded Sky glanced at Iron Maiden. Seemingly oblivious to the conversation, she turned where she stood, staring at every detail of the scenery from the carved birds and tigers on the corners of the monastery roofs to the tumbled, rocky hillside below the courtyard parapet.

"We've already fought them once." It seemed she had been listening after all. "We would have done it again, but they were too frightened and ran away! With your help, Elder, we can fight them again and this time destroy them."

Harmonious Virtue blinked at her.

"Miss—er—"

"They call me the Iron Maiden," she said, cupping her fists.

"Miss Iron, Old Tze has said, 'I make no effort—and the people transform themselves.' Wudang Sect was founded

61

for the purpose of enlightenment and spiritual cultivation. We do not involve ourselves in political disputes."

Iron Maiden blinked.

"Do not fear," Harmonious Virtue added. "For the same reason we cannot allow the emperor's men to enter the gates of this monastery. If necessary, I will go out and speak with them. So far from Nanjing, with the gates of Wudang closed against them, there's little they will be able to do."

Iron Maiden still seemed confused. Clouded Sky added quickly, "*Shifu*, Iron Maiden has come from the other side of Hubei looking for someone to go with her to Ten Thousand Thorns Temple."

Harmonious Virtue raised his white eyebrows. "Miss Iron, do you think there is truth in that old legend?"

"Truth? I know it's true. I've been there myself."

"You have *been* to Ten Thousand Thorns Temple?"

She nodded.

"Humble self was not able to wake the princess from her meditations. I have been searching the martial arts world for one who can! Perhaps one of Wudang Sect's disciples can help."

"To wake the princess?" Harmonious Virtue stroked his beard. "Miss Iron, how does an enlightened one return to the ordinary world? A broken mirror never reflects again. Fallen flowers never go back to the old branches."

Iron Maiden's brow creased in momentary concentration.

"What about an attachment to what is beyond one's self, Elder? Do you think that would do it?"

Harmonious Virtue looked at her for a little while.

"How old are you, if this decaying one might ask, Miss Iron?"

She dropped her gaze sadly.

"This ignorant one does not know, Elder."

Harmonious Virtue spoke in a very gentle voice.

"A wise answer, Miss Iron. Now you are able to answer any question."

"I have heard it said that the sea cannot be measured with a bucket, *shifu*." Clouded Sky wasn't sure why he was defending her, but he spoke before he could stop himself. "Iron Maiden is not so ignorant as one might think! Her martial skill and internal force are profound. She has defeated me twice."

Iron Maiden looked at him gratefully, and then bowed to Harmonious Virtue.

"Try me, Elder! Let us exchange stances, and see for yourself if my martial arts are any good!" She lifted her palms.

Harmonious Virtue stepped back hurriedly and said, "Once on a tiger's back, it is hard to alight, Miss Iron." While Iron Maiden thought about this, Clouded Sky realised the old priest was looking at him, weighing him up. At last Harmonious Virtue added, "Miss Iron, you must be weary after your long journey. Someone will show you to the guest house now, and tomorrow morning,

I will introduce you to our disciples. Perhaps one of them will be interested in helping you." He paused. "Although I must warn you. I am unsure whether you will find any Wudang Sect Disciples willing to mend the broken mirror, or return the fallen flower to the branch."

Iron Maiden bowed, cupping her fists.

"Still, I will speak to them, Elder."

Harmonious Virtue bowed and clapped his hands, whereupon a young disciple crossed the courtyard to escort Iron Maiden to the guest house.

When she had gone, Harmonious Virtue laid the spear-box on the parapet next to him and slid back the lid. For a while he looked down on the broken spear, his lips moving in prayer.

As the sun sank into the west, the light began to fail.

Finally Harmonious Virtue looked up. "I perceive that you have not agreed to go to Ten Thousand Thorns Temple, Clouded Sky."

"No. She asked me and I refused."

"Why is that, my disciple?"

He kept no secrets from his *shifu*. "I know I must return to Mount Jing. The Emperor is busy with the Yuans in the north, but once he is free to turn his attention to Hubei again, he will come to destroy the last of the Roaring Tiger troops. I must remain focused on the greater good, and not allow Iron Maiden to turn me aside."

Harmonious Virtue bowed his head. "Who is this Iron Maiden? Who is her *shifu?*"

"I don't know, but I do not think her martial arts are completely orthodox. She has a variant of Wudang Sect's Heaven-Shaking Palm Technique, but far more aggressive."

"Hmmm. A fierce dog ruins a liquor shop, my disciple."

Clouded Sky considered this for a moment. If he kept bad company, it would drive away his true friends. After a moment his *shifu* continued.

"Remember, Wudang Sect occupies a position of honour in the martial arts world. Even though you have completed your training, you should be careful not to 'bring injury to the group.'"

"I know, *shifu*. But with the Imperial Guard following us, I thought it was better to stay together."

"Surely there was someone else you could join forces with."

"So I thought, but there's a price on my head. With Roaring Tiger dead, no one was willing to defy the Emperor." He sighed. "I didn't just come here to return Broken Spear's weapon, *shifu*. I've become concerned about my martial arts. Worthless self was always a poor student. I can't even exchange stances with one young maiden, let alone a troop of imperial guards. Now the time has come for me to take Broken Spear's place. Please, Elder, give me more training before I return to Mount Jing."

"My disciple, those who know when they have enough are rich." Harmonious Virtue's words held gentle rebuke.

"Yes, *shifu*, but learning is a weightless treasure you can always carry. I was happy to be second after Broken Spear. But now he is gone, and I realise I can no longer be content as I am." Clouded Sky put out a hand to touch the broken weapon as he tried to contain his sorrow. "Before he died, Broken Spear told me his dream of peace in All-Under-Heaven. No more massacres. No more broken families. Broken Spear entrusted that dream to me. It is my duty to carry it forward and see that it comes true."

Harmonious Virtue stared into the sunset, now little more than a lemon-yellow streak under lowering purple clouds. "That dream is what made Broken Spear the great martial hero he was. It would have brought him to perfect enlightenment, in time." His eyes slanted sideways to Clouded Sky. "You understand that victory is not the ultimate goal for a warrior."

"Yes, *shifu*."

"We learn the sword so that we may understand that we are one with the sword. This is a noble discipline. But once this is attained, there is a further path to take. Here, we understand that we are one with all around us. Not only the sword, but also the man at the other end of it. When we understand this, we reach enlightenment and lay down the sword."

"You have taught me this from my youth, *shifu*."

Harmonious Virtue nodded.

"As you have foreseen, the Mount Jing rebels desire you to lead them. Since the death of Roaring Tiger, they do not have a leader. Roaring Tiger's son is too young. Three days ago, an emissary arrived, saying they had heard a rumour that you had escaped and were making your way here. It seemed impossible—and yet, you have returned."

"Roaring Tiger envoys? Here?" Clouded Sky turned from the parapet in delight. "Who came?"

Harmonious Virtue gave another sigh, a long wistful sigh that quenched his happiness.

"*Shifu?*"

"Two tigers cannot live on one mountain, disciple."

Harmonious Virtue meant that he was being distracted by two different purposes. "That is true, master." Clouded Sky bent his head. "But please, let me dedicate myself to your teaching for as long as I can. Two months or so."

"Two months! Surely it is the shallowest stream that runs most swiftly."

"I could stay longer." Clouded Sky swallowed. "But without my help the Emperor will take Hubei, and Broken Spear's dream will fail."

There was a short silence. Softly, Harmonious Virtue said: "I also have a dream. I am growing old. Soon Wudang will need a new Sect Leader. It is a task for a young man, but it requires a high aptitude. Of course, I had already picked out a disciple to replace me. Together with my martial brothers, we had chosen Broken Spear to be Sect Leader after my death.

"Now that he is dead, I agree with you that it is time for you to take his place. Perhaps also as Sect Leader, when I die."

Clouded Sky restrained the questions that rose to his lips. He forced himself to remain silent a while before he selected one in reply. "*Shifu*, you confer on me a great honour. Did Broken Spear know you had chosen him as Sect Leader?"

"No." Harmonious Virtue looked sadly at the spear box. "If he had, perhaps he would still be here today."

"Do you think he would have been content to study spiritual matters here at Wudang, with All-Under-Heaven suffering war and chaos?"

"He would not have forgotten the ultimate goal of a warrior."

Spiritual enlightenment. Not victory over the Vastly Martial Emperor.

"Truly, virtue grows one foot while evil grows ten feet," Harmonious Virtue went on after a moment. "The time when martial artists could roam the world freely, righting wrongs and doing justice, is past. Most people are willing to submit to the Vastly Martial Emperor. As chaos overpowers All-Under-Heaven, the righteous submit to the will of Heaven. The eagles return to the mountains, the tigers to the forests, and the sages to the fortress of their own convictions."

For a long time Clouded Sky could not find the words to speak. Clearly, Harmonious Virtue thought he should abandon the Roaring Tiger troops to their fate and dedicate himself to the continuation of Wudang Sect.

Harmonious Virtue was unquestionably a venerable and wise counsellor, but his heart rebelled every time he imagined telling the Mount Jing emissary that he would never return.

At last he cupped his fists. "*Shifu*, will you allow humble disciple to depart? You have given me many things that are difficult to understand. Please allow me the time to think this over and make the right decision."

Harmonious Virtue bowed.

"A teacher may open the door, but you must walk through it yourself. Take as much time as you need, my disciple. And here." He handed Clouded Sky the broken spear in its wooden box. "Take this with you. It may help you to clear your mind."

* * *

A disciple led him to his lodgings. Clouded Sky was surprised to see that they went toward the disciples' quarters, not toward the guest house, but he was glad to see his old cell again. It seemed more like a homecoming.

He sat down to meditate, but once more he found it difficult to clear his mind. Worry assailed him. Was Harmonious Virtue right? And whether he was right or not, wasn't it his duty as a disciple to obey his master?

Yet it was impossible to contemplate Harmonious Virtue's advice without emotion. For three years he had fought beside the Roaring Tiger troops. He knew the stories. The Emperor had slaughtered thousands of subversives, displaced whole towns and caused thousands more to starve. Everyone had lost a child, a sibling, or a spouse. The thought of giving up the fight made him feel ill.

If this was the Way, he now understood why some repudiated the Way and resorted to dangerous and unorthodox martial arts.

He shook himself. Such thoughts were in themselves dangerous! Perhaps, fighting with Roaring Tiger, he'd become too attached to the illusory world. Or Iron Maiden had infected him with her heresies. If he was to be Taoist Priest Harmonious Virtue's successor as Wudang Sect Leader, he could not allow himself to be distracted like this. Clouded Sky closed his eyes, determined to put Roaring Tiger and Iron Maiden out of his thoughts.

It took him a long time to clear his mind to the point that he could begin to meditate. Then, just as he found the necessary clarity, *crack! crack!* Something rapped against the shutters of his room.

A bird? A mischievous disciple? He forced his jolting heart to slow and closed his eyes again, but the sound returned, an insistent *rat-tat-tat* that gradually increased in force.

Finally he got up and yanked the shutters open.

"Why disturb me? Why not just let yourself in?" he snapped.

Iron Maiden hung upside-down from the gutter above,

her face pink and smiling. "I wanted to be polite, Clouded Sky *dage*. You might have been asleep."

With her around? Unlikely! He swallowed the retort, and stood back as she slipped through the window.

"Why are you here, Miss Iron?"

"They wouldn't let me in by the door. No women in male disciples' quarters."

"That's correct. You should go, heroine."

"But I needed to see you and they wouldn't take a message." Her brows knitted. "They said, 'Go back to your quarters, Miss Iron. Martial brother Clouded Sky is not here.' I wonder why they lied."

"How did you know I was here?"

"I followed you when you came."

"You *followed* me?" *Again.* Clouded Sky took a breath. "Miss Iron, you can't do that. People find it very disturbing. *I* find it very disturbing. Please, will you go back to your quarters? I need to meditate."

Clearly his manners were deteriorating under her bad influence. For a moment he hoped she might be offended and go away. But of course, her only response was to plant herself on his sleeping mat and clasp her hands loosely across her knees, making the room hers as easily as she had made his horse hers. "I was thinking about Taoist Priest Harmonious Virtue. What's he going to do about the imperial guards?"

"Didn't you hear, Miss Iron? He'll speak to them and send them away."

"I know, I just saw him go out the gate to meet with them. But what if they don't listen?"

"They'll listen. Taoist Priest Harmonious Virtue knows what he's doing; he's settled worse troubles than this. He'll convince them to leave us alone."

"What if they don't listen? What if they attack?"

"Don't be afraid, heroine!"

She laughed. "Who's afraid? I know you and I can fight them together, *dage*. That's why I'm staying here till your *shifu* comes back."

Clouded Sky swallowed. "Heroine, you can't stay! I'll lose so much face if anyone finds out you've been here. Don't worry. Even if the Imperial Sword was mad enough to attack, all of Wudang Sect would help us fight back!"

"Would they? Taoist Priest Harmonious Virtue said Wudang Sect must not fight the Emperor's troops."

"Well, you heard him say that Wudang Sect is not political. Spiritual cultivation is the true goal of a warrior! But you can trust my *shifu*, heroine. For years, he's helped the Emperor's enemies escape to Tibet. It's not his job to fight the Emperor, but that doesn't mean he won't help us if we're attacked."

"Elder, you know him better than I do. But what if he's wrong about the goal of martial arts?"

It was Clouded Sky's turn to laugh. "Taoist Priest Harmonious Virtue, Wudang Sect Leader, is *wrong* about martial arts?"

Iron Maiden looked down at her feet, blushing. "A poor

child who is wise is better than an old and foolish king who will not hear instruction, *dage.*"

Clouded Sky could not contradict this. "So how is my *shifu* wrong about martial arts?"

She sat silent for a moment, thinking. Then she smiled, and jumped onto the window-sill.

"Come with me, and I'll show you."

Before he could reply, she launched herself from the window and soared through the night air, the white sleeve of her dress rippling in her wake. Clouded Sky sighed. At least if they went elsewhere to talk, they would no longer be breaking the rules.

He followed her in a series of shorter leaps that took him past the temple and the courtyard where they had spoken to Harmonious Virtue, over the roofs of the guest quarters and up the mountain to a small level area that he knew well. Covered with fine gravel and carefully weeded, it was the training-ground where he and Broken Spear had spent hours exchanging stances as disciples.

Below them the monastery lay silent and peaceful, and beyond it the mountainside plunged into soft strands of fog, from which other hilltops emerged like islands in the sea. In the moonlight, the earth itself glowed like a lantern.

Iron Maiden backed away from him across the gravel. "You have your sword? Good!"

In a cranny of the mountain a bamboo clump was growing. Iron Maiden used her knife to cut a thin, flexible

73

cane and trim the leaves. Then, gripping it by the end, she took her stance: knees bent, two fingers of her left hand raised behind her, and the bamboo cane pointing like a sword at his heart.

It was a stance he knew. Clouded Sky drew his sword warily. "Wudang Sect Soft Snow Swordplay?"

She didn't answer. She just kept her eyes on him, a smile lurking in their depths. Then she attacked.

It was like all their other duels. For a short time Clouded Sky understood and thought he could predict her stances. Then suddenly, she executed an attack of incredible speed and power, one he had never learned and could not comprehend at all. The bamboo slipped past his sword and halted within a whisper of his death acupoint. Clouded Sky stared at the quivering green tip and held his breath. Iron Maiden straightened and adopted another stance he knew.

"Again, *dage*."

It was always humiliating to be so easily defeated. But this time, more curious than offended, he paid closer attention to what he was doing. This time, one of his feints fooled her, piercing her guard, but she slid aside like water, and he felt the sting of bamboo across his neck.

She straightened, watching him. In her eyes he could see the earth and sky reflected: the white moon, and the banks of white fog.

He thought he was beginning to understand.

"Again," he said.

74

They closed. Iron Maiden's stances were fluid and adaptable. When he struck, she retreated. When he retreated, she advanced. Although he wielded a quick sword, she was never there when he struck. Instead, her bamboo cane twisted and danced where his did not. And whether she advanced or retreated, she kept the bamboo's end flickering about him, looking for an opening.

Back and forth they maneuvered. Again he was able to predict many of her stances—all of them from the various Wudang Sect sword styles. Then—he had begun to expect it by now—in the midst of a stance he thought he knew, she changed direction and caught him on the wrong foot. As she laid the point of her green sword against his chest, her eyes willed him to understand.

"Again," he said.

This time he stayed on the defensive, letting her come at him fast and deadly. Letting her show him what she meant to show him.

Then he saw his chance and moved, a feint with the sword. She bent backwards to avoid it and his leg swept her feet from under her. She flipped onto hands, then back to feet, but his face was there to meet hers as she straightened.

His fingers against an acupoint on her neck.

He looked into her eyes again and saw fright. Surprise. And then, unexpectedly, laughter.

"You *did* it!" He didn't expect her to look so delighted now that he'd finally defeated her. "Clouded Sky, *dage*, you did it!"

He stepped back, sheathing his sword. "Heroine's martial arts are just like mine—Wudang Sect sword styles. But yours take more opportunity to attack. And all your attacks kill or disable."

"Exactly! While yours merely threaten and retreat."

Her dismissive words goaded him.

"Why not? Martial arts is about avoiding a fight as long as possible."

"It is good to preserve peace. But what if you are already in a fight? These are the *martial* arts we are talking about, not the making of tea! If one is in a fight, one attacks to win!"

"Tea? What do you mean?" Clouded Sky shook his head. "Wudang Sect prizes the virtue of mercy."

"And victory?"

"That is not a proper consideration. A martial artist does not fight to win victory."

"Of course one must fight for justice even if there is no hope of winning! But where is your reliance on Heaven? And these martial arts of yours!" Iron Maiden smacked the bamboo stick against the ground in disgust. "Why don't you go back to your Mount Jing troops, and tell them what you have just told me? 'My friends, victory is not a proper consideration for us, and therefore I will not learn any martial arts that will help me to gain victory over the Vastly Martial Emperor. I will make only a pretense of fighting him so that I will not feel bad when he takes your land and starves your families!'"

"How dare you!"

"I'll tell you what I think. Fighting the Emperor makes you feel good about yourself, but actually defeating him—that would mean finding some other way to bring order and peace to All-Under-Heaven. I think you're afraid of winning. What would you do if you actually defeated the Emperor? How would you deal out justice? How would you ensure peace?"

"How can I give answers to such questions?"

"If you don't, someone else will! Or maybe you're afraid that if the Emperor was defeated people would stop putting their trust in you, obeying you, and giving you money? Maybe with the Emperor gone, they'd need a different kind of hero. A man of peace, a wise man, not a warrior—and they wouldn't need *you* anymore."

Clouded Sky opened and shut his mouth several times before he found the words to speak. "You can talk all you like, Miss Iron, but all I can do is my best. If the Emperor really does have the Mandate of Heaven, there's nothing I can do about it."

Iron Maiden swept up the bamboo stick and gave him a stinging cut to the knee.

"Don't be foolish! If the Emperor truly had the Mandate of Heaven, we would know it! We would know it because he would act according to the righteousness of Heaven, rather than committing these horrible crimes. Is Heaven pleased when people starve because corrupt officials take all their grain? Is Heaven pleased when the Emperor kills and relocates people just to force them into submission? Is this really the Mandate of Heaven? Or is it your own cowardice?"

Too angry to speak, Clouded Sky grabbed the bamboo stick and yanked it out of her hand. Iron Maiden let go unconcernedly and walked past him to the edge of the cliff.

"Your Sect Leader has returned." She didn't turn her head to speak to him. "I suppose it's safe for us to sleep. If you won't think about what I have said, *dage,* then think about what you have learned fighting me."

With that she lifted her arms and stepped off the edge of the cliff. For a moment she floated down through the moonlight, arms spread, her gown and sleeves rippling. Then she disappeared into the shadows at the gate of the guesthouse, and he knew she was gone.

"I, a coward!" he huffed as he tramped down the narrow steps along the cliffside toward the disciples' quarters. Arrogant and foolish peasant! Couldn't she see that her excessive love of justice would only result in harm to everyone? The worst of it was that she stirred up unseemly emotions in his own heart. Clouded Sky took deep, slow breaths in an attempt to soothe his temper. At least he could comfort himself with the thought that he'd finally defeated her in a fight.

But only by using one of her own stances.

Doubt like a night traveller crept into his mind.

Clouded Sky did not return to his room at once. Instead, weaving his way through the shadowed pathways of the monastery complex, he went a little way beyond the disciples' quarters and emerged in a courtyard near the monastery gate, overlooking the south hills.

He unsheathed his sword and began to move through the stances of Wudang Sect's Mystical Sword Style. For the first time since his early days as a disciple, he paid close attention to every movement.

He executed three stances and stopped. Then, eyes closed, he moved through the stances again, this time imagining an opponent before him.

He took a stance, and attacked. Took a new stance, and attacked. Took another. And attacked.

He opened his eyes again, the cold night air drenching his lungs at each breath. Was she right after all? Could these stances be used for offence in ways he had never imagined?

Was his sword style really faulty?

Iron Maiden's fighting style was uniquely savage and effective. There were plenty of unorthodox martial artists in the world: low lives and followers of evil cults, despised by all righteous heroes. The Venomous Palms of the Yin Winds, for example, and the Black Stone Assassins. These were martial artists who never restrained themselves from any atrocity at all. Who fought only to kill.

Was Iron Maiden one of these?

And yet—his feet led him through another stance. His sword swept and flashed, releasing a burst of internal force that made the shutters rattle on the nearby buildings. Clouded Sky stood motionless, listening to the night, his heart beating.

What if someone saw him?

There was a power here that terrified him. Quickly, he returned his sword to its sheath and turned toward his quarters. As he crossed the entrance courtyard, a flutter of motion caught the corner of his eye. He turned, narrowing his eyes into the shadows.

The monastery complex was walled and gated. Was it only his imagination, or had he seen a silent shadow drop from the wall above the gate?

In the blackness under the roof of the gatehouse a thin crack of light slowly appeared. There was a soft groan of hinges. The streak of light grew and was choked by a sudden flow of shadows.

"Intruders!" Clouded Sky shouted the alarm at the top of his voice and dashed for the gate, his sword seeming to leap into his hand.

Where was the gatekeeper? Immobilised? Dead? There was no time to wonder. A gang of twenty men wearing dark night-travellers' outfits stepped into the moonlight. With a muffled word of command they suddenly disappeared in twenty different directions, using their lightness skill to scale the walls and roofs.

One man remained behind, drawing his sword and taking his stance. The faint moonlight failed to illuminate his face. He was wearing a mask.

The Imperial Sword!

Clouded Sky launched himself into the air. "You dare to breach Wudang Monastery? Eat my sword!"

The swordsman reacted with breathtaking speed, leaping into the air and lashing out with his blade. Clouded Sky's own sword stroke went wide, and a stinging pain scored his flank. Clouded Sky landed and turned, pressing his hand to the shallow wound. It came away slippery with blood. For a moment he looked into the Imperial Sword's masked face. Then the swordsman turned and ran.

Clouded Sky shouted again and leaped after him, attacking so hotly that the Imperial Sword was forced to turn and face him. Despite his best efforts the emperor's sword flickered faster than his own, and with each movement Clouded Sky felt hot blood seep from his wounds. His strength was already failing—and this opponent effortlessly blocked all his strikes. Although the Imperial Sword used stances and sword styles from a number of different sects, Clouded Sky could tell he was also familiar with Wudang's techniques, able to predict each of his own stances.

In desperation he unleashed one of Iron Maiden's sudden, devastating attacks. His sword whistled through the air, converting a feint into a lunge. The masked man's eyes widened and he dropped to the ground, sweeping a leg around to trip his opponent. Imperial Sword saved himself by a hair's breadth, and threw Clouded Sky to the ground.

Clouded Sky jumped back to his feet, his heart pounding so hard he thought it would burst. The Imperial Sword, however, did not press his advantage.

"You're wounded," he rasped in a whisper. "Give up, or you will be freed from illusion tonight!"

Clouded Sky only laughed and attacked again. Once more, he changed his direction partway through a stance and launched an unpredictable attack. The Imperial Sword gave a grunt of surprise and shifted clumsily to block the attack, but the black sword was too heavy and too powerful for his slim, supple sword. There was a flash of internal force and the Emperor's sword broke with a sharp, flat *snap*. The black sword bit into the Imperial Sword's upper arm.

The masked man seemed barely affected by the shallow wound as he leaped into the air and soared onto the nearest rooftop. Clouded Sky's lightness skill was not so profound. He dashed away in the same direction, searching for a path up, keeping his eyes fixed on the shadow flitting across the rooftops. A railed entrance on one side of the alley gave him his chance. He leaped from the ground to the rail, from the rail to the wall opposite, and rebounded from the wall to the rooftops.

Not far ahead the Imperial Sword raced toward the

temple area. Clouded Sky stooped as he ran, snatched up the roof-tiles, and hurled them after him. Tiles sang and cracked all around them. The masked man launched himself from the roof and sailed directly across the temple courtyard.

Clouded Sky reached the edge of the roof just as the moon vanished behind a cloud. Darkness fell on Wudang Mountain.

Under a glowing lantern on the far side of the courtyard, Harmonious Virtue stood in a small huddle with his martial brothers: Taoist Priests Venerable Peace, Filial Thoughts, Incipient Favour, Loyal Prudence and Leaping Intellect. In the disciples' sleeping quarters to Clouded Sky's immediate left, more lamplight showed as shutters creaked open and curious faces peeped out. But the Imperial Sword had vanished into the darkness.

An ancient woman, no doubt one of the travellers fleeing to the monastery for refuge, got up from the verandah near the priests and hobbled painfully across the courtyard. Her stick clacked loudly against the stones until she reached the foot of the temple's high terrace and laid herself down again with a rusty sigh.

It was a scene of peace and tranquillity, the night silence undisturbed, as though no one had heard his cries for help, as though the imperial guards had been no more than ghosts. Yet the wound in his side proved it was not an illusion.

Clouded Sky let himself down into the courtyard and

ran to his sect elders.

"*Shifu!*"

Harmonious Virtue turned toward him.

"Clouded Sky? Ah—I'm glad you're here."

"Sound the alarm," he panted. "Snow Wind is here. I think he's after Iron Maiden!"

He tried to pass them, aiming for the guesthouse, but to his amazement, Harmonious Virtue's staff swept out and caught him by the ankles. Clouded Sky crashed to the ground and rolled over with a groan of pain. At once, six uncompromising feet landed on his chest, pinning him to the ground. He looked up into a ring of stony faces.

"My disciple," Harmonious Virtue said calmly, "it is unwise to create wind and fire before all facts are known."

Clouded Sky stared at him uncomprehendingly. Then, slowly, he began to understand what he had seen. An unguarded gate. Peace reigning even after his shouts to raise the alarm. Sect disciples looking out at their windows, hearing the commotion but keeping to their cells.

Iron Maiden, complaining that when she asked for him they told her he was not there.

"Everything is under control," said Taoist Priest Leaping Intellect.

"No," Clouded Sky whispered. "You couldn't…"

In the distance a commotion suddenly arose. It was the sound of battle: shouts, grunts, the wind of powerful palm and sabre strokes. Clouded Sky tried to push off

84

the ground.

"Please! They're going to kill her!"

Harmonious Virtue removed his foot from Clouded Sky's chest and kneeled to look him in the eye.

"No, my disciple. They are not going to kill her, any more than we will allow them to kill you."

Clouded Sky searched his *shifu's* face.

"You let them in," he whispered.

"One cannot pour oil without tipping the bottle, Clouded Sky. Sometimes a little disruption is necessary to achieve a desired goal."

"But *why?*"

Harmonious Virtue lifted a hand and the Sect Elders stood back. When he had helped Clouded Sky to his feet, the priest stared at the pavement for a while, as if collecting his thoughts. Finally he sighed and lifted his head.

"My disciple, the Vastly Martial Emperor has the Mandate of Heaven. It is our duty to assist him."

Chapter 3.

The Mandate of Heaven?" Clouded Sky looked at his *shifu* in horror.

"It is our duty to obey the emperor's commands since he is placed over us by Heaven. Iron Maiden has defied Heaven and broken the emperor's law."

"So did I! Are you going to hand me over to them?"

"No, no—"

"Why not? There's a price on my head too! Does Heaven want you to turn me in? What about the Mount Jing troops? Where does this end?"

"As long as the emperor does not require us to commit personal unrighteousness—"

Distantly, a shriek of pain rose into the sky. Iron Maiden.

Clouded Sky groaned and grabbed at his sword.

"Please, *shifu*, there's no time..." He tried to break through the encircling elders, but Harmonious Virtue repelled him with a palm strike to his chest.

"My disciple, Miss Iron has raised tigers and made trouble for herself."

"But they'll kill her. Please, *shifu!*" He was begging now, tears in his eyes, willing them to listen. To spare him the burden of this choice.

"They have promised not to harm her," Harmonious Virtue said quickly.

"They promised? *I* promised she would be safe here!"

"It was not a decision we made lightly," put in Taoist Priest Leaping Intellect.

"She will indeed be safe. That was part of the agreement," Harmonious Virtue added.

"You ought to be more grateful!" said Taoist Priest Filial Thoughts. "They wanted you as well! It was only by promising them that you would neither intervene, nor leave this temple for the next year, that they agreed to let you live."

Clouded Sky's voice cracked.

"You would keep me a prisoner?"

"Disciple! No!" Harmonious Virtue held up his hands appealingly. "We will not keep you anywhere against your wishes, but we beg you to remain. If you leave you will die. If you stay you will live, and I can die with confidence that Wudang Sect will continue under your leadership."

Clouded Sky felt that he was being torn inexorably in two pieces.

"Continue? What for? Why should we continue, when we have failed to do justice, to help the needy, and to rely humbly on Heaven?"

"Clouded Sky! You speak disrespectfully!" Leaping

Intellect scolded him.

"Hush, martial brother," said Harmonious Virtue. "Clouded Sky is concerned for his friend. But hear me, young disciple. How have we lost our purpose? No matter who holds the Mandate of Heaven, Wudang Sect *must* continue guiding disciples toward heavenly enlightenment. Only then will All-Under-Heaven experience a small amount of peace, prosperity, and harmony!"

"*Shifu,* you were the one who taught us to rely on Heaven in all things." It was as though everything he had ever believed had turned to sand and was flowing away from his grasp. "Are you saying now that we can't win?"

"Disciple, Old Tze has truly said, 'Give evil nothing to oppose, and it will disappear by itself.'"

"If that were true, then how can it be the duty of every righteous hero to punish injustice?"

Harmonious Virtue bent his head. Sadly, he said: "Although one can understand the truth, sometimes one just can't bear it."

Clouded Sky closed his eyes in utter bewilderment. If this was truly the Way, then only two choices were left to him. Either he must watch as they dragged Iron Maiden into captivity. Or he must abandon enlightenment, righteousness, and Heaven itself. Another cry of pain split the air. In that piercing call for help, he found the one solid thing that he could trust. Clouded Sky opened his eyes and cupped his fists.

"Honoured *shifu*, you have convinced me. The true Way is to stand by and do nothing." He took a ragged breath. "Please accept humble disciple's apologies. I can no longer live my life according to your teachings."

"Clouded Sky! No! If you do this it will be the end of Wudang Sect!"

"The Emperor will destroy us!" Filial Thoughts added.

"I suppose he knows best." Clouded Sky stepped backward, looking for a way out of their encirclement. "After all, he was appointed by Heaven!"

"Foolish child! Listen to your masters!" Leaping Intellect lifted his hands. Hidden projectiles hissed from pipes hidden in his sleeves.

Clouded Sky threw himself backward, deflecting the darts with his sword. Taoist Priest Incipient Favour grabbed a whip made of linked blades from his belt and uncoiled the razor-sharp lash toward him. Clouded Sky twisted to avoid the blades. The whip flickered about his body, forcing him to dance like a phoenix to avoid it. In a moment, he saw his chance and struck with his sword, severing the whip as he would a venomous snake.

He straightened, breathing hard, and found that he was still surrounded by Wudang Sect's six elders. All of them had drawn weapons. Leaping Intellect held hidden-projectile pipes in each hand. Incipient Favour swung his truncated whip. Venerable Peace carried paired hooks, while Loyal Prudence, Filial Thoughts, and his own master, Harmonious Virtue, had drawn their swords.

How could he defeat them all?

"*Shifu*, please let me pass!"

"Iron Maiden has a wolf's aggression and a dog's bark," Harmonious Virtue said sadly. "We promised we would allow no interference."

They waited. In the silence, Clouded Sky could no longer hear the sounds of battle from the guesthouse. Desperately, he flung himself at Leaping Intellect, unleashing one of the ferocious sword stances he'd discovered watching Iron Maiden's sword style. It was a feint stance, but he followed it through with an attack. His sword flashed with energy as it flickered out, stabbing the priest's *Heaven's Gate* acupoint. With a scream of pain, Leaping Intellect crumpled to the stones.

Clouded Sky froze in horror.

"Martial uncle! Are you all right?"

At once he felt a killing aura flame out behind him. He twisted just a moment too slow. Loyal Prudence's sword opened a long shallow cut on his shoulder at the same moment that Venerable Peace's hooks caught and held the blade of the black sword.

Clouded Sky swung his sword, pivoting around to put Venerable Peace between himself and the other elders. With both hooks grappling Clouded Sky's sword, Venerable Peace was unable to defend himself properly from the kick Clouded Sky unleashed at his chest, even as he twisted the sword between the twin blades. *Crack!*

The hooks shattered in a blaze of sparks and Venerable Peace flew through the air.

Clouded Sky had no time to incapacitate the old priest further. His remaining martial uncles adopted the Four Pillars formation, two of them attacking, two defending. Two of the swordsmen, Loyal Prudence and Filial Thoughts, attacked in unison, their swords singing in the wind and flashing with energy. Meanwhile, Incipient Favour and Harmonious Virtue, one with his shortened whip and the other with sword, focused on blocking all of Clouded Sky's attacks.

Fighting in formation, the four priests were unbeatable. Even the small enlightenment Clouded Sky had gained fighting Iron Maiden would not avail him. The Sect Elders' martial arts were subtle and devastating, the very zenith of Wudang Sect ability. Step by step, they forced him backward across the courtyard and toward the temple steps.

Blood seeped from Clouded Sky's wounds, weakening him further with every movement. He could no longer contemplate attack. As his energy drained, it was all he could do to defend himself. When he blocked one sword, another threatened. The end could not be far.

Then it came.

Loyal Prudence struck from his left, and Clouded Sky jumped aside to evade the sword. His foot caught on something and he fell sideways into the shadow of the temple's high terrace.

Right on top of something soft, which squawked when he fell.

It was the old lady he had seen crossing the courtyard not long before, now curled up to sleep. As he rolled away she gave a cry of outrage, got to her elbow and lashed out with her staff. With a ringing snap, Loyal Prudence's sword broke in two pieces.

"Oh, how dare you!" the old lady cried. "Did no one ever teach you young people to respect your elders?" She rose panting to her feet. "What do you Wudang Sect Elders mean by ganging up on this young man? *I* heard you! Mandate of Heaven, indeed!"

"Old Madame." Harmonious Virtue bowed in deference to her greater age. "This is a matter of Wudang Sect discipline. Kindly step aside!"

"Step aside? Nothing would give me greater pleasure! Unfortunately, I have a message for you from Heaven."

"A message from Heaven?"

The old lady gave a brisk nod. Then she launched into the midst of them with her staff humming like a dragonfly. *Crack! crack! crack! crack!*

She sank into a crouch, her staff tucked under her right elbow, two fingers of her left hand extended.

There was a sound like heavy rain as weapons and Wudang Sect Elders fell to the ground.

With a quick motion the old lady stood up, set her staff on the ground, and leaned on it—once again seeming to be a harmless beggar. Clouded Sky gaped.

"Well, clumsy? What are you waiting for?"

"Honoured madame! I thank you!" Clouded Sky cupped his fists, and then ran for the guesthouse.

He pelted through a narrow alleyway on the far side of the temple courtyard and emerged into the courtyard facing the guesthouse. Immediately he saw signs that a terrible battle had taken place. Light streamed out of a window whose shutters had been burst open. Outside, some of the paving-stones were shattered with the force of palm or weapon strikes. Three imperial guards in night-travellers' outfits lay dead on the ground.

Scraps of white fabric from Iron Maiden's sleeves littered the pavement. When Clouded Sky picked up one of the pieces, he saw in the faint light that it was dark with blood along the torn edge.

One leap took him through the broken window into the lamplight beyond. Clearly, the battle had begun here. The room was a wreck, littered with smashed pottery and splintered wood. Even the stone pillow had been lifted from its place and hurled at an enemy. Now it was embedded deep within the wall.

There was no sign of Iron Maiden.

Clouded Sky stood motionless, clenching the bloody scrap of fabric in his hand. He had failed. Again. Now, because he hadn't listened to her, because his martial arts were not good enough, another of his friends was in the hands of the Emperor.

Something scuffled behind him. He turned with a wild

sword swing, but the blade skipped ineffectually off a staff.

It was the old lady from the temple courtyard.

"They took her," he gasped.

"Perceptive." The old lady raised an eyebrow. "What are you going to do about it?"

"Do about it?" he repeated stupidly. The next step had not even entered his mind yet. He was only just beginning to realise how exhausted he was, how painfully his wounds ached in the cold. "What *can* I do about it?"

"Go to Ten Thousand Thorns Temple to finish her quest."

"Go to—no! I don't know the way. *Shifu* promised Iron Maiden would be kept alive. I have to find her first."

Thwack! The old lady's staff rapped him painfully on the ankle.

"The function of the mind is to think! Must I do it all myself? Go west, to Ten Thousand Thorns Temple. That's where they'll be taking her."

"Why?" There still seemed to be a fog of exhaustion in his mind. "Do they want to wake Princess Morning Light too?"

The old lady stared at him. And then it dawned on him.

"They want the Heaven-Relying Dragon-Slaying Sword Skill! They want the Golden Phoenix Sword!"

"If Morning Light is permitted to return to the martial arts world, it may be the end of the Vastly Martial Emperor's wars in the west! Of course they want to reach her first."

"And they'll keep Iron Maiden alive long enough to find the Temple." Clouded Sky wiped his sword and returned it to its sheath. "All I have to do is follow them!"

He rushed out of the guesthouse. The old lady listened to the echoes of his retreating footsteps, then settled herself under the verandah for a nap.

* * *

The sun rose that morning into a clear sky, sending golden shafts of light and shadow streaking through the tree-trunks. Just south of Wudang Mountain it ran between the legs of horses and stole through the bamboo bars of a cage mounted on a cart.

With each movement the cage squeaked, and a pattern of shadow and light wavered over the unconscious shape inside. Iron Maiden. The sun ran careful fingers over her pale cheek and found an answering warmth under her skin. It tiptoed gently over the blood staining her dress and illuminated the slow breath which fogged the crisp morning air.

Then the cart passed under the trees and it lost her.

Perhaps it was the sudden cold that woke her. Iron Maiden groaned and shifted. Watching from his mounted vantage-point, the Imperial Sword readjusted the mask that covered his face and directed his men to turn aside under the trees.

95

When the cart stopped Iron Maiden groaned again, gingerly pressing a hand to the gash across her ribs. Despite the pain stabbing through her body, she pulled herself up to a sitting position.

A white horse tethered behind the cart huffed welcomingly.

"Flying Crane?" she murmured, then looked up at the Imperial Sword. "You stole Flying Crane!"

"I have the emperor's personal authorisation to take whatever actions seem necessary, Miss Iron." The Imperial Sword dismounted, unhooked a waterskin from his saddle, and held it toward her. "Are you thirsty?"

She didn't want to admit it, but after a moment she nodded.

"Good. Then maybe we can drive a bargain." The Imperial Sword hooked the waterskin back onto his saddle and stepped closer to the bars. "You, heroine, know the location of Ten Thousand Thorns Temple."

Iron Maiden tried not to let any flicker of emotion cross her face, much less an indication that the Imperial Sword was right. He didn't wait for an answer.

"You do. I can see it in your eyes."

"I'll never tell you."

"Please, Miss Iron, don't be unreasonable. You need food and water. Blankets. Medicine for your wounds. Tell us where to find Ten Thousand Thorns Temple and we'll make sure you have everything you need."

"And what if I don't? Will you starve me?"

The Imperial Sword would not look her in the eye.

"I must carry out the Emperor's orders, Miss Iron. A word, and you can end your sufferings at any moment. Everything you need is here. I am begging you to accept it."

Iron Maiden gathered herself painfully onto her knees, the better to peer through the bars at him.

"Why do you want to find Ten Thousand Thorns Temple?"

"They say the Golden Phoenix Sword is there. Morning Light is meditating, perhaps dead. She does not need the sword."

"Why do *you* need it?"

At first there was no answer, and Iron Maiden wondered if the Imperial Sword was going to respond at all. Finally he said, "I am new in the Emperor's service. There are crimes in my past for which I must atone. The Vastly Martial Emperor wants the Golden Phoenix Sword as a sign that he has inherited Coiling Dragon King's authority and heroism. Once he has the sword, Hubei and Sichuan will submit to him of their own free will. And I will earn a full pardon."

Iron Maiden kept her hand pressed to the wound across her ribs. The effort to remain upright made her feel light-headed and nauseous. When she did not reply at once, the Imperial Sword continued.

"The Emperor means to bring back order and peace to All-Under-Heaven. It is my duty to make that happen."

A wave of dizziness passed over her, and her vision darkened. Iron Maiden grabbed the bars of the cage. Her strength was ebbing. She must act now.

"Will you help us?" The Imperial Sword's voice seemed to come from a distance.

"Help you?" She fought back the dizziness and looked up into his eyes again. "To steal Morning Light's patrimony and give it to the beast emperor? Never!"

"Heroine, I'm begging you to reconsider."

Iron Maiden closed her eyes and for a little longer she sat in the blue-grey morning shadow, breathing slowly and deeply through flared nostrils, her mouth drawn tight against the pain and sickness that assailed her.

Then she moved.

With a shout, she hurled one tremendous palm strike at the bamboo of her cage. The air filled with splinters.

Her second blow was a jab aimed at the Imperial Sword's *Spirit Storehouse* acupoint, but her wounds made her slow and weak. The Imperial Sword blocked the blow with his sheathed sword, then countered with a quick jab here and a pinch there.

Her acupoints sealed, Iron Maiden slumped backward into the broken cart with shallow, distressed breaths. The Imperial Sword pushed his hood back to wipe his forehead.

"Put her in fetters."

Quickly, two of the guards brought a massive wooden fetter. With the Imperial Sword muttering at them to make haste, they quickly fastened the heavy block around Iron Maiden's neck and wrists. Others brought new bamboo poles to repair the cage. As soon as they were done, he massaged her acupoints until she awoke.

Iron Maiden groaned.

"If I die," she whispered, "you'll never find Ten Thousand Thorns Temple."

"Don't worry, Miss Iron." He stepped back, wiping his hands on a napkin. "I would never allow you to die."

The words were anything but a comfort.

* * *

His horse was gone.

A cave at the foot of Mount Wudang served as a stable for visitors to the monastery. Since it was not convenient for the priests or disciples of the monastery to keep riding horses, Flying Crane had only had three donkeys, an old and lazy pony, and five horses as his companions, which much have belonged to travellers.

Now all of them were gone, the gate to the cave torn off its hinges, and the keeper of the stable nowhere to be seen.

The moon had fallen behind the hills while Clouded Sky fumbled his long way down the mountain stairs, and by the time he had reached the cave it was too dark to follow the Imperial Sword's trail any further. In any case, neither he nor they would have been able to hunt forever without sleep. Clouded Sky had put medicine on his wounds, wrapped himself in his cloak, and despite the evening's events, quickly fell asleep.

He was awakened early in the morning by a creaking sound.

It sounded as though it had come from the gate at the mouth of the cave, and when he sat up, he could see it wavering on its hinges. Stiffly, Clouded Sky got up and went out of the cave, but there was no sign of any visitor. Instead, some distance away, five persons hurried down the mountain. When they saw him, they began to wave and shout.

"Honoured brother Clouded Sky! Wait for us!"

It was the Mount Jing emissaries. After everything that had happened last night, he'd forgotten they had been at Wudang waiting to speak to him. Clouded Sky met them with delight.

"Red Cloud! Old Sunlight and Madame Sunlight! Fortunate meeting!"

Old Sunlight cupped his fists and bowed, his face crinkling in smiles. "Fortunate indeed! When we heard that you had already left Wudang, we did not know if we would catch you in time!"

"In time? Is there something wrong?"

"You must return with us to Mount Jing at once, kind elder brother," Red Cloud burst out. "Since the death of Duke Roaring Tiger, we have had no one to lead us. And now there is news that the Emperor's war in the northern

100

provinces is over! His armies will be in Hubei before winter's end. We need you to prepare us for the war!"

Hopeful faces surrounded him. Clouded Sky nodded slowly.

"I will come and help you. Soon. Perhaps before the new moon. But there's something I have to do first."

Their faces fell.

"We are in terrible disarray," Old Sunlight pleaded.

"Then I'll finish my mission and return to you as soon as I can. Last night…" He couldn't bring himself to explain every detail of Harmonious Virtue's treachery. "Last night some imperial guards broke into Wudang and captured a martial heroine, my friend, Iron Maiden. They are taking her west into the mountains. She relied on my word that she would be safe here; she has saved my life once or twice already. Honour prevents me returning to Mount Jing without her."

"But what are we going to do?" Red Cloud asked.

"You'll have to return to Mount Jing and set things in order yourselves." Clouded Sky turned to Old Sunlight. "Everyone respects you, Elder! Tell them that I have appointed you to gather the troops and fortify the strongholds."

"Respected young friend!" the old man stammered. "How can this old and decaying one bear such a responsibility?"

"Because there's no one else to do it, that's how!" Madame Sunlight spoke for the first time. "Don't worry, young friend! We can carry out your orders."

"But don't be long," Red Cloud added.

"I'll come as quickly as I can. This Iron Maiden is a peerless martial heroine. If I can bring her to Mount Jing, perhaps she will teach us the secrets of her profound martial arts—or at least help us in the fight against the emperor!" He hesitated. "But first I have to find her. The emperor's men have stolen the horses."

"No!" Red Cloud ran to the cave and looked inside. "Where's the keeper?"

"Who knows?"

"They wouldn't have taken the donkeys with them," Red Cloud said thoughtfully. "Perhaps they also left some of the horses." At once, he put his fingers in his mouth and gave a piercing whistle.

After a moment, the sound of hooves rumbled through the forest, and the missing five horses trotted onto the road, followed more slowly by three donkeys and the pony. Red Cloud caught the best of the horses, and led it to Clouded Sky. "Please, honoured elder brother, accept this miserable animal. I will walk home if I must."

It was no Flying Crane, but it would carry him faster than he could go on his own feet. Before Clouded Sky rode away, Old Sunlight bowed to him.

"Come back quickly, young respected friend."

* * *

The Imperial Sword was a man of his word. Every few hours he called the march to a halt, and while the men eased their thirst or stepped into the forest to relieve themselves, he reached into the cage to satisfy himself that Iron Maiden still lived. She lay limp and unmoving on the floor of the cart while stinging flies walked the crusted wounds on her body.

"You have a fever, Miss Iron," he told her at midday. "Best you give up your information and allow us to help you."

She did not respond. Had she even heard him? The Imperial Sword signalled for the march to begin again, telling his men to eat their noon meal in the saddle. The Taoist priests had promised to keep Clouded Sky on Wudang Mountain, and Second Brother had remained behind to watch the mountain, still determined to collect the bounty. Nevertheless, it was best to travel fast and leave Wudang as far behind as possible. By the time the sun set and Imperial Sword called a halt, everyone was exhausted. Iron Maiden lay shivering uncontrollably in the cart.

It should have been impossible for anyone to catch up with them but just as they seated themselves by the campfire to eat their evening meal, a rustle in the tree-tops announced an intruder.

The Imperial Sword jumped to his feet with his sword drawn as a man dropped lightly out of the branches.

"Second Brother! What are you doing here?"

"Clouded Sky has left Wudang, your excellency. I came to warn you."

"He's coming here?"

Second Brother nodded. The Imperial Sword took a slow deep breath. Skilled, observant, and officious, Second Brother had quickly become a thorn in his side.

"And you let him come? You were supposed to capture him and take him to Nanjing!"

"The Emperor wants him alive, and I can't do that if I must take him all the way to Nanjing by myself. Best we join forces, your excellency."

"Impossible."

Second Brother made himself comfortable next to the fire.

"No, really, your excellency. It *is* best. You already know that I'm highly skilled. With my help, you can make it safely to Ten Thousand Thorns Temple, retrieve the Golden Phoenix Sword, capture Clouded Sky, and get back to Nanjing alive." He paused. "It would be a shame for the Emperor if your mission failed."

In the light of the fire, Imperial Sword read Second Brother's face and manner. Once again, he felt uneasy. Was the bounty hunter threatening him?

The reason for the man's insistence wasn't difficult to guess. Like everyone else, Second Brother had heard of the secrets of Ten Thousand Thorns Temple. Clearly he was no longer as interested in the bounty on Clouded Sky's head as he was in Morning Light and the Heaven-

Relying Dragon-Slaying Sword Skill.

Still, Second Brother had been helpful so far, and might be again. Especially if Clouded Sky was now following them. The Imperial Sword moved his arm gently, feeling a twinge where Clouded Sky had cut him. He couldn't force Second Brother to take Clouded Sky to Nanjing. Perhaps they needed the help. Perhaps it was best to have the crafty bounty hunter where Imperial Sword could keep an eye on him. At least for now.

"Very well. We accept your help."

In the cart, Iron Maiden whimpered in pain.

"Is that Miss Iron?" Second Brother helped himself to a bowl of rice. The Imperial Sword looked toward the cage.

"She needs help."

"Your excellency should let her suffer."

"If she dies, we may not find Ten Thousand Thorns Temple until it's too late."

Imperial Sword left the firelight, unlocked the cage and gently turned the girl onto her side. Closing his eyes, he placed both hands against her back and began to circulate his *qi* energy, forcing it through his hands and into Iron Maiden.

His hands grew warm. Iron Maiden's shivering slowed and finally stopped as the healing energy flowed into her, battling the poison in her wounds and pushing back the effects of hunger, thirst, and exposure.

She gave a deep sigh and murmured, "Clouded Sky?"

At once he removed his hands from her back, breaking the flow of energy. As he locked the cage, she dragged herself into a sitting position and stared at him with a face as pale as a ghost.

"Better now?"

She moistened her cracked lips and whispered, "Just kill me."

His *qi* infusion had restored her dying body, but it could not have relieved the pangs of hunger or thirst, and he could see that it had not healed her wounds.

"I know this must be hard for you. Please, heroine, I want to help you."

She closed her eyes.

"Mouth of honey, heart of daggers."

"I do. In all sincerity."

She smiled faintly in reply, and he leaned forward, gripping the bamboo cage. How could he explain that he was in earnest?

"I have a sister too. It causes me pain to think of her suffering like you."

"Free me, then. I would never wish to cause you pain."

He pretended not to notice her sarcasm.

"Forgive me, Miss Iron, but you know I can't do that."

There was a little silence. After a moment, her eyes flickered open again.

"Do you think you're a righteous man?"

The Imperial Sword stood speechless. He *was* a righteous man. He served his country and his emperor to the

106

best of his ability. He never allowed himself to become angry. He always considered the good of others before his own. When fighting, he restrained himself. He meditated often. He cultivated respect for his elders and humility before heaven. Because of his quest for righteousness, he had given up everything that had once mattered to him. It was unfair of this girl to ask him a question like that. For a moment he allowed himself to lose a temper which he had guarded tightly for many years.

"Are you hoping for Clouded Sky, heroine? Don't put your reliance on him. Even if he escapes Wudang, there are bounty hunters after him. You won't see him again." He paused, waiting for her response, but she made no answer, and with her eyes closed again, there was no way to know if she was listening. "Miss Iron should also know that we know that Ten Thousand Thorns Temple is in Sichuan, in the mountains. Whether you decide to help us now or not, we will certainly find it sooner or later. We are in no hurry."

"Then why did you steal Flying Crane?"

Through the dusk he saw Iron Maiden smiling again, but whether the sharp curve of her lip was mockery, pain or some terrible mixture of both, he didn't know. The Imperial Sword took hold of the bamboo bars of the cage and spoke very quietly.

"Perhaps Clouded Sky will come. But if you care for his life, you should pray that he does not."

Nevertheless, as he returned to his men, the question

still jangled in his mind. He pushed it away. Yes. Yes, of course he was a righteous man. After all, he was only following orders.

Back at the campfire he found the firelight playing like a funeral-blaze on the faces of his men. Second Brother looked at him, his face as blank and unreadable as ever.

"I gave her a *qi* infusion," Imperial Sword said. The moment he spoke he knew the words were a mistake, an admission of weakness.

Sure enough, Second Brother took advantage of it. He poked the fire with a long stick.

"The girl will never talk if you treat her too well."

"She's sick, hungry, and thirsty. She'll talk."

Second Brother snorted.

"Anyone can bear that. If she can stand a day of it, she can stand a month of it. You need to let me frighten her." He withdrew the stick from the fire. The end of it was a glowing coal, and he looked meaningfully at the Imperial Sword.

"No," he said on pure reflex.

Slowly, Second Brother stood up. His eyes were only on a level with the Imperial Sword's shoulder, but there was no awareness of disadvantage in his eyes.

"With the deepest respect, your excellency, we're wasting time. We need her information and we need it fast, before she gets well enough to escape or sick enough to die."

Do you think you're a righteous man? Under his mask,

the Imperial Sword moistened his lips.

"I have rules."

"You have orders, your excellency."

He couldn't be having this argument right now. Not in front of the men—which was probably why Second Brother had chosen this moment for a confrontation.

"I thought your excellency was on this mission to prove your loyalty," Second Brother added.

"And I will. Who are you to tell me how I should obey my orders, Second Brother? After all, I was given considerable latitude in carrying them out." He tried to show a confidence he didn't feel. "One way or another, Iron Maiden will give us what we want to know."

Second Brother looked at him thoughtfully. Imperial Sword sensed the man's challenge. He slid his left hand down to the Emperor's sword, thumbing the catch on the hilt, refusing to blink an eye. Of course, the Emperor's sword was broken, and if his bluff failed everyone would know. He held his breath and waited for the flame of a killing aura.

Instead, Second Brother lowered his gaze.

"Your excellency knows best. But if she hasn't said anything within two days, I say we do it my way. Remember, most of the people in these parts would rather die than submit to the emperor. If we don't find the temple soon, we may never live to find it at all."

There was a faint murmur of assent from the men.

"I agree, your excellency," one of them said, emboldened

109

by Second Brother's words. "We're between a mountain of knives and a sea of fires out here. Please, let's find out what the girl knows and put her in the ground."

The Imperial Sword hesitated, but he sensed he wouldn't get any better reason out of them.

"Two days, then."

He didn't rejoin the men around the fire. Instead he walked a little way apart, trying to calm his thoughts.

Do you think you're a righteous man?

All he wanted was peace under Heaven. He'd counted the cost. He'd determined to pay it. But he wouldn't compromise any further than he had to. So far as he could, he vowed he'd keep his hands clean.

* * *

Once again, Iron Maiden woke to the healing warmth of a *qi* infusion. Once again, the Imperial Sword ended the treatment long before she'd had enough, leaving her alive but tormented by thirst and hunger, the crusted wounds on her chest throbbing with fever. When he was finished, the Imperial Sword locked the cage and circled around to look at her.

"Is there anything else I can do, heroine?"

"You can stop mocking me. Even when he wants to show mercy, a wicked man is cruel!"

The masked man leaned closer.

"Heroine, please consider the possibility that I may not

be wicked. I've been sent to retrieve the Golden Phoenix Sword for the emperor. That's all. Where is the harm in that? Why suffer all this for such a little thing?"

"Because the Golden Phoenix doesn't belong to you!" She glared at him from behind the ragged curtain of her hair. "And because I know what the so-called emperor will do with the sword once he has it! He will bathe it in the innocent blood of thousands."

Imperial Sword's eyes fell. "One cannot pour oil without tipping the bottle. Because of all those who refuse to recognise the Mandate of Heaven, peace cannot come to All-Under-Heaven without bloodshed."

"Including my blood?"

Still he wouldn't meet her gaze. "Those who resist the emperor's righteous intentions have only themselves to blame. They will always be permitted to lay down their weapons and obey him."

"Is that what you've done?" She dragged herself onto her knees, trying to ignore the pain. "Look at me. Look me in the eyes. Do you find honour in serving this self-styled emperor, then?"

He obeyed her command and looked at her, but not to answer the question.

"I'm here to make an offer. Lead us to Ten Thousand Thorns Temple, and then come back to Nanjing with us. There is nothing the emperor will refuse to the woman who offers him the Golden Phoenix Sword. Not just your freedom, but money, station, anything you might care to name. Even appointment as his concubine."

Better to be a broken piece of jade than an unharmed brick. Better to die with honour than live in shame.

There was no point in saying it, so she kept silent.

"Heroine, I have to warn you." His voice sank even lower. "It's imperative that we know where to find Ten Thousand Thorns Temple, and soon. My men are fearful and growing impatient. Unless you tell us what you know before tomorrow night, I must allow them to question you themselves."

His eyes were haunted, his voice earnest. She felt the cold certainty that he meant it.

"What is it to you, anyway, heroine? If the emperor has the Mandate of Heaven, nothing you do can stop him. My men are desperate to return home safely. If they fail, they die. If they succeed, they win a magnificent reward and the emperor's forgiveness for the crimes in their past. We are looking for redemption, Miss Iron. The emperor will have the Golden Phoenix sooner or later, but we only get one chance to put ourselves right with him. So do you."

"Put myself right with him!" She clenched her fists until the wooden fetter bit into her wrists. "Let him hang between Earth and Heaven three days, and then I will put myself right with him. But not before."

The Imperial Sword stepped back, shaking his head.

"You have until tomorrow night. I implore you, don't make this hard for yourself."

He cupped his fists and departed to saddle his horse. As he left, Flying Crane was led up to be tethered behind the cart. Iron Maiden stared into the liquid eyes of the only other being in this camp that would sympathise with her in her captivity.

There was a thump. The whole cage shook. Iron Maiden jumped. The man leading the horse looked through the bars with an ugly sneer.

"Tomorrow night, Miss! His excellency will be taking a *long* walk."

Her heart raced, leaving her sick and faint, but Iron Maiden tried not to let her terror show on her face.

All that morning she lay in the bottom of the cart with her eyes shut, shivering from her fever. At first she tried to circulate her *qi*, but it was a losing battle. She was too sick and weak to heal herself, and it was only the Imperial Sword's infusions that kept her alive.

What could she do?

The hours passed like a nightmare. She paid no attention to her surroundings until the cavalcade lurched to a stop and the Imperial Sword unlocked the cage again. He eased her out of the bamboo cage and supported her to the grass by the roadside. They stood near the summit of a high hill on the borders of the mountains. The wind was cold, the sky a pearly cloud and below them for looping miles the road lay like a raw noodle on the hillside.

Far below, a solitary horseman plodded up the road.

"Heroine was right." The Imperial Sword spoke as

calmly as ever. "He has followed us."

The horseman's head was bent, but she could see the handle of the sword on his back, and the swinging red tassel which hung from its hilt. Iron Maiden felt life flooding back into her.

"Clouded Sky!"

Her voice perished in the wind, unable to reach him. In the same moment there came the sound of horn and cord groaning. Iron Maiden looked up to see one of the guards draw a bowstring to his ear. The short, curved bow was as thick as her wrist, the arrow wickedly barbed. It would fly fast and do incalculable damage.

She stopped breathing. The Imperial Sword looked down at her.

"Where is Ten Thousand Thorns Temple, heroine? Tell us. Or he dies."

Despite herself, a whimper escaped her throat.

"No!"

"Is the Golden Phoenix Sword really worth your friend's life?"

Iron Maiden wept without tears; all the moisture in her body was dried up. Despite his arrogance, Clouded Sky was the only person who had been kind to her for longer than she could remember.

"I don't believe you," she said at last.

"What don't you believe, heroine?"

"That you only want the sword. What good is a sword to the Emperor? No. He will kill Morning Light, and the

114

Heaven-Relying Dragon-Slaying Sword Skill will be lost forever!"

There was a moment's silence.

"The Emperor means no harm to Morning Light. Our orders are only to retrieve the sword. I swear it, heroine. None of us will touch the princess."

Maybe he was telling the truth. And maybe he wasn't.

"You are willing to murder my friend. Why should I believe you about the princess?"

"Make your choice, heroine! Speak now, or your friend dies."

She looked up at him.

"It's your choice, not mine. If he dies, you'll never find Ten Thousand Thorns Temple. I'll never tell."

The Imperial Sword's eyes narrowed. Then he dropped his hand. At his signal, the bowstring sang.

"No!" Iron Maiden screamed. The effort was too much for her; there was a sudden roaring in her ears, and night fell on her vision.

When she awoke, she was in the cage again, and the endless march continued.

* * *

Night fell and the cart finally stopped moving. It was bliss to Iron Maiden. After being bumped over every rut in the poorly-kept road, she ached from head to foot. Her head pounded, the fetter chafed her neck, and because of her great thirst she had been unable to shed even one tear for Clouded Sky.

Was he dead? Was she truly alone?

The Imperial Sword came to give her another *qi* infusion, but this time he remained in the cage much longer than usual. When he finally removed his hands from her back, she felt better than she had in days.

"Can you walk?"

She was surprised to find that she could. With the Imperial Sword's help she climbed stiffly out of the cage and saw that they had stopped in a small town. Light glowed from the door of a tavern where the guards went in and out. A man in the blue robes of a minor official bowed low to the Imperial Sword and led them down the street.

Iron Maiden looked around the street in curiosity. Where was she? She clenched her fists inside the wooden fetter. If she could get her hands free, could she strike a blow for freedom? Could she overcome the ten guards that surrounded her?

They stopped, and the official bowed again.

"The prison, your excellency!"

It was a small building containing no more than two or three cells, all of them empty, but Iron Maiden's hopes plummeted at the sight of its massive posts and bars. As the imperial guards shoved her into the nearest cell she yanked helplessly at the fetter, but her feeble strength was not enough.

"Is there anything else we can do for you?" the official asked anxiously as the prison keeper entered Iron Maiden's description into his book by the flickering lamplight. "Your excellency is the emperor's personal envoy!"

"My men are tired and need rest," said the Imperial Sword. "Can I trust you here to watch the prisoner?"

"Yes, of course. And anything else? You will tell the revered emperor that we did everything in our power to assist?"

Their voices faded away down the street, the official still laying every amenity of his town at the Imperial Sword's feet. Evidently, some in the western provinces hoped to avoid the emperor's wrath through early submission.

Iron Maiden hadn't had the chance to ask what had happened to Clouded Sky. She bent her head, fighting back despair. Two guards watched outside the lockup, two more in the dim lamplight within. Maybe if she broke her thumbs she could slip her hands out of the fetter. But it would expend too much *qi* energy to heal them. After that, there was no way she could fight her way past the bars that hemmed her in, or the guards, or the town gates. She could not fight her way out, and she was not clever enough to scheme or bargain her way out.

For a hundred years Morning Light had meditated in peace, waiting for her day to come. Once more Iron Maiden vowed that she would never betray the princess, but what if the unthinkable happened? What if they found a way to break her will?

A soft sound came from outside the lockup. Iron Maiden stiffened. That sounded like a fist! But that must mean...

Inside the lockup the two guards looked at each other and tightened their grip on their spears. Cautiously, one of them edged closer to the door.

"Who's there?"

No answer. Which meant that the sentries outside must be gone or incapacitated.

Iron Maiden held her breath as the two guards stepped outside. For a moment, nothing happened. Then it was as if one of the very shadows had come to life. There was the sound of two blows, almost simultaneous, and both the guards crumbled to the ground with a faint chime of weapons.

Their attacker leaped into the lockup.

He wore a black night-traveller's outfit and a mask. But a red tassel swung from the hilt of his sword.

"Clouded Sky!" Iron Maiden whispered.

"Heroine! Are you all right?"

She puffed strands of hair out of her eyes and nodded radiantly.

There was a whisk of movement beyond the door. "Behind you, *dage!* Imperial guards!"

Clouded Sky whirled, unsheathing his sword and attacking in the same motion. It was impossible to see anything, just a red flash as the sword left its sheath. Then the foremost attacker's head toppled to the ground a moment before the rest of his body.

Two more guards immediately forced their way in, one on either side of Clouded Sky. Iron Maiden rushed toward the bars and watched with her lips parted, shackles forgotten. Clouded Sky's sword flickered in both directions, stabbing and piercing. But trapped in a narrow space between two assailants, he was unable to see both attackers at once. As he pressed one back, the other aimed a swordpoint at his back.

"Behind you, *dage!*" she yelled. Clouded Sky reversed his sword and struck behind without looking. The attacker fell to his knees grasping a stomach wound. "In front! Use your fists!" Iron Maiden shouted. Clouded Sky stepped forward, feinting with his left fist and attacking with his sword-weighted right.

Suddenly, the night was silent again.

Clouded Sky turned on his heel and unlatched the heavy door of the lockup.

"*Yellow Fisherman Hauls the Net? Guan Yu Heavy Fist?* The perfect stances, heroine!"

"So that's what they're called."

"Did they hurt you?"

Still beaming, she shook her head.

"Can you ride?"

"If you take this thing off."

"Hold still, then."

His sword struck the shackle between her neck and wrists. The wooden pieces split and Iron Maiden extended her arms with a sigh of relief.

"I feel better already! What about Flying Crane, *dage?*"

"I've already got him." Together, the two of them rushed out into the night.

At once shouts split the air. The Imperial Sword ran from the tavern at the head of his men. Clouded Sky whistled, and Flying Crane emerged from an alleyway, surging into a gallop. He vaulted into the saddle and Iron Maiden alighted behind him, catching hold of the saddle with a laugh of pure joy.

* * *

Clouded Sky allowed himself to breathe more freely once they left the town. His plan was a hasty one, invented as he went along, and he'd had no way of knowing if the guards he bribed would keep the gate open past sundown as asked. To his relief, all went smoothly. Once safely outside the town wall, he turned off the road onto a narrow path running into the forest.

Iron Maiden had been silent since the lockup, her fingers linked on the cantle of his saddle, her head occasionally bouncing on his shoulders with the gait of the horse, as if fighting slumber or exhaustion. Now she spoke.

"Where are we going?"

"Not far, heroine."

"I thought they shot you with an arrow, *dage*."

"They missed me, but killed my horse. I had to buy another from a manor-house." Later he'd used the second horse to bribe the town gatekeepers. Thoughtfully, he added, "The Imperial Sword doesn't seem the kind of man to miss what he aims at. Did they kill the horse on purpose?"

"The Imperial Sword threatened to kill you if I didn't tell them where to find Morning Light. Maybe he changed his mind. Maybe he thought you'd be more useful alive than dead."

"A hostage for your good behaviour? Maybe so." He thought for a moment. "I suppose that means you told them to go ahead and shoot me, heroine!"

"If a person does wrong, he alone must take the blame. Your life would have been lost for a noble cause, *dage*."

It wasn't quite the answer he had hoped for.

"Why are we going towards the moon?" Iron Maiden's voice was dreamy with exhaustion. "Ten Thousand Thorns Temple is the other way."

"Because we're going here instead." Flying Crane ambled to a stop. "Look, heroine. This is where we'll spend the night."

It was an ancient ruined manor house, hidden in a valley and overgrown with creepers. Discreet questions at the manor where he bought the horse had suggested this would be a good place to hide. He could only hope that the Imperial Sword would not make similar inquiries. After the excitement of her escape, Iron Maiden's strength was clearly ebbing. Clouded Sky helped her inside and quickly found a still-intact room where some traveller or bandit before them had left a stacked pile of firewood.

Warmth, food, water, and the salve he'd brought in his saddlebags soon revived Iron Maiden's strength. He returned to the room just as she finished bandaging her wounds.

"You thought of everything, *dage*."

"I knew you would need the medicine. I saw the scene of the fight at Wudang. Oh! I had forgotten." He dug into his saddle-bags again and brought out a tiny box ornamented with white cranes.

"My tea!"

"You left it at Wudang."

She pulled off the lid and breathed in its aroma with tears in her eyes.

"Tea, 'the beverage that quenches thirst, and dissipates sorrow.' Clouded Sky, *dage*..." Her voice trailed away.

He wanted her to go on. He wanted her to express the thoughts which brought that light of gratitude and admiration to her eyes. But she restrained herself, and a look of sadness quenched the light briefly before she straightened with a dutiful smile.

"Thank you, *dage*. I should be able to travel in the morning. Ten Thousand Thorns Temple awaits!"

Clouded Sky settled down cross-legged beside her.

"That's what we need to talk about, heroine. We can't go any further. In the morning, we must return to Mount Jing."

Her face fell. "But I thought…"

"You were wrong."

When Iron Maiden was taken from Wudang, Clouded Sky had come to realise how profoundly he respected and even loved her. But who would act as his matchmaker for her? They were alone on a desperate mission. Now, hesitantly, he smiled. "I didn't come in search of Ten Thousand Thorns Temple. I came for you, *meimei*."

As soon as the word left his mouth, Clouded Sky held his breath. Calling her *little sister* like that was too flirtatious. But to his relief, she blushed and looked down shyly.

"Clouded Sky *dage*, if you hadn't come, I think I would not have survived. Thank you."

He opened his mouth to speak again, but she said quickly, "*Dage*, listen. If I had died, my secret would have died with me. On the road, in that cage, I decided that the secret must be shared! I must tell you the location of Ten Thousand Thorns Temple."

"Me?" Clouded Sky stared, distracted from his thoughts of love. "But I'm nobody."

"You, hero, are the only person I can trust."

Could she? He thought of what she had endured, and wondered if he would have been so courageous in the face of such danger and deprivation. But she went on:

123

"Six days' journey west of here is a place named Pine Settlement. North of Pine Settlement one day's journey is a hidden valley in the mountains. That's where Ten Thousand Thorns Temple is."

Closer than he thought. As if reading his mind, she said: "Surely we can spare the time!"

He shook his head. "I promised them at Mount Jing that I would come back as soon as I found you, so that you could teach us martial arts. The Emperor is coming to Hubei with an army. Help us defeat him first, then we'll travel to Ten Thousand Thorns Temple together."

She looked at him in dismay.

"Teach you martial arts? *Dage*, I can't! I've already taught you everything I know."

"But, heroine! You said you would teach me!"

"You are a quick learner, *dage!*" She nodded. "I only had one principle to teach, and within a short time you have already grasped it!"

"How can this be when your martial arts are so far above mine?"

"Perhaps they are. But it's no use, because I can't teach them." She touched her lips nervously with her tongue. "You asked me who my *shifu* was. The truth is, I don't know. I can't remember anything that happened to me before the spring of this year."

He stared at her, speechless. Then he drew his sword. With a flash of light it sliced toward her neck. Iron Maiden's eyes widened. She threw herself backward.

One foot rose in a smooth arc, turning aside Clouded Sky's wrist and slamming it against the floor with a dull clatter. Then she was upright again, palms lifted to strike. Slowly, carefully, Clouded Sky raised his left hand in a gesture of peace.

"That. What you just did. How did you do it, heroine? What do you call it?"

She lowered her palms and released his sword hand.

"I don't know, *dage*. Until you drew your sword, I didn't know I could do it. I never do."

Clouded Sky sheathed his sword and buried his face in his hands, trying to think.

"It's as I told you." She seemed almost about to cry. "I am only an ignorant girl. I cannot teach anyone what I know, because I don't know it myself. If you want to improve your martial arts, you must let me take you to Ten Thousand Thorns Temple."

Clouded Sky stared into the fire.

Iron Maiden looked down at her hands and sighed. "It will be like pulling a tooth from a tiger's mouth, *dage*. I understand if you don't want to go."

"It's dangerous?"

"Last time I barely escaped with my life. But two are twice as good as one, and if we go together, we might succeed." There was a short silence. "With the Imperial Sword searching for the temple too, there's no time to find someone else."

Clouded Sky sighed. He'd promised Red Cloud and

Old Sunlight that he'd hurry back, but he had to face the facts. The Mount Jing rebels were not enough to face the Emperor in full force, and his martial arts skill was not profound enough to make up the lack. He needed Morning Light. He needed the Heaven-Relying Dragon-Slaying Sword Skill. No matter what danger he must face to find it.

"There's no need to find someone else, heroine. If you really want me, I'll go with you to Ten Thousand Thorns Temple."

* * *

Beckoning a lantern-bearer to stay close, the Imperial Sword mounted the steps of the lockup and looked down at the guards' crumpled bodies.

Second Brother was on his knees inspecting their wounds.

"No one saw the rescuer's face, your excellency. But he was evidently using a Wudang sword skill, and he took Flying Crane when he left."

"Clouded Sky." The Imperial Sword seemed thoughtful.

Second Brother got to his feet. "They must also pass the city gates."

"I sent a messenger."

The two men stepped into the street. They did not have long to wait before a guard in red-and-black livery hurried around a corner and came toward them. Bowing, he said, "Iron Maiden went through the east gate. She's left the city."

The Imperial Sword closed his eyes and let out a long breath. Then he smiled coldly at Second Brother. "You see? A hen forced to nest does not lay eggs, Second Brother! My plan is working."

"So far, your excellency."

"You saw the girl. She never would have talked. Or if she had, she would have lied. There's no sure way to break that kind of resolve. But now she'll lead us of her own accord, and she'll lead us right."

"What happens when they realise we are following them to the Ten Thousand Thorns Temple?"

"They won't notice that I had the horse reshod. Flying Crane will leave distinctive prints, and with your skill in tracking there should be no trouble finding the trail."

Second Brother looked impressed.

"It is as I said," Imperial Sword added. "The Emperor's vision of peace and unity in All-Under-Heaven must be achieved with minimal bloodshed. The way of justice and mercy is always the best way."

"Perhaps you are correct, your excellency. But take pity on this ignorant one's confusion." Second Brother smiled tightly. "Did the Emperor not command you to kill Morning Light?"

Imperial Sword tried not to allow any suspicion to show in his face.

"The imperial orders are a matter for the Imperial

127

Sword. They are not your concern, Second Brother!"

But Second Brother continued.

"According to the prophecy, Morning Light is soon fated to wake from her meditations. She alone knows the secret of the Heaven-Relying Dragon-Slaying Sword Skill. When she awakes, she will certainly claim the Coiling Dragon King's authority. The emperor would never send you all this way simply to retrieve the Golden Phoenix Sword! Morning Light *must* be the real target!"

The Imperial Sword suppressed his dismay. Second Brother was only trying to test him again. "I've received no such orders. Return to the inn, Second Brother. You have no more to contribute here."

And yet…

Before he left Nanjing the Emperor had given him sealed orders—orders he was only permitted to open once he had located Ten Thousand Thorns Temple. Now, he had to wonder what could possibly be inside them.

"Go back to the inn," he told Second Brother a second time. When the bounty hunter reluctantly started toward the tavern, Imperial Sword grabbed the lantern from its bearer and carried it into the lockup, reaching into his tunic for the sealed orders. With fingers that shook slightly, he broke open the seals and unrolled the scrap of silk.

Written in red ink was a warrant for the execution of Princess Morning Light.

As the Imperial Sword stared in consternation, the

128

step to the lockup creaked. He turned, covering the silk with his hand, but it was too late. Second Brother had glimpsed the blood-red ink that could only mean death, and although he didn't smile, he radiated satisfaction.

"So there must be a little bloodshed after all, your excellency. Too bad for justice and mercy!"

Chapter 4.

Iron Maiden had healed quickly from her ordeal. Captivity had sharpened her appetite, and food rapidly replenished her stores of *qi* energy. On the third day she began to use her lightness skill. Instead of riding, she floated through the treetops as fast as Flying Crane could run. For three more days the road led them through a landscape of forests and increasingly high mountains split by deep valleys. Sichuan seemed to be enjoying a fragile peace: unhurried merchants and farmers passed by, secure in their humble poverty or the strength of their hired escorts.

They came to Pine Settlement on a grey evening that threatened snow. A poor and squalid cluster of huts squatting beside a broad lake in a stony bed, Pine Settlement had little in it but fishing-boats and a timber mill.

"There's not even an inn," Clouded Sky realised as they reached the end of the village and saw the lonely road climbing into the mountains ahead of them.

Iron Maiden was perched on Flying Crane's hindquarters behind him. Undaunted, she pointed eagerly to the path ahead.

"That's the way to Ten Thousand Thorns Temple, *dage!*"

"The weather looks bad. We'll try it tomorrow, hero-ine." Clouded Sky turned Flying Crane back toward the village. As he did so, a solitary figure in a black cloak turned aside into the shadows between two houses.

Iron Maiden caught her breath.

"Did you see that?"

Clouded Sky nodded.

"We saw the same man last night at Bright Moon Settlement."

"He's following us." Iron Maiden's voice sank to a dismayed whisper. "No, no, no! We can't afford to lead anyone to Ten Thousand Thorns Temple!"

Suddenly decisive, Clouded Sky spurred Flying Crane into a trot toward the mountains. Not far up the moun-tain road, the path looped around a spur of rock. With a glance behind, Clouded Sky turned Flying Crane behind the spur and dismounted.

They did not have long to wait. The man in the black cloak hurried up the road on their trail. Iron Maiden fell from the rock above him. He heard her movement and turned with a yell of surprise, reaching for the hooks he carried at his belt. Too late! With one jab to an acupoint, he fell to the ground. Clouded Sky left his hiding-place, rolled the man over onto his back, and gave a grunt of surprise.

"I know this man! He was at the tavern when we first met."

"He's with the Imperial Sword, *dage*. They call him Second Brother. The others can't be far away." Her eyes widened in dismay. "What have I done? I've led them straight to Morning Light's door!"

"Don't blame yourself, heroine. It can't be helped now." Clouded Sky stood and whistled to Flying Crane. "All we can do is go on and reach Ten Thousand Thorns Temple before they do! What will we do with Second Brother?"

"Put him under the rock and leave him. He would need truly wonderful *qi* cultivation to wake up before morning, and by that time we'll already be at the Temple." Her eyes sparkled. "At last!"

Clouded Sky did as directed, then turned to find that Iron Maiden had slipped into his saddle and held Flying Crane's reins. She barely waited for Clouded Sky to vault onto the horse before stirring Flying Crane into a gallop.

Neither of them looked back.

Neither of them saw Second Brother rise to his feet and run toward the village.

* * *

At first the road ran straight into the mountains, but a little further on it began to wind to and fro, always rising up the steep hillsides. Below them the lake contracted to a fast-moving river and above, the path narrowed to a ledge on the side of a cliff.

"Heroine, slow down!" Clouded Sky shouted as they approached a hairpin turn.

"I know every step of the way, *dage*! It's not far now!" Iron Maiden turned Flying Crane and went on with reckless confidence up the mountainside. The stones dislodged by the horse's hoofs tumbled down a fathomless distance into the gorge. Clouded Sky tried not to hear them. White flecks of snow blew in the wind, punctuating the thick clouds darkening the sky. Flying Crane dropped from a trot to a walk, his sides heaving.

"How much further, heroine?"

"Not far!" She slid out of the saddle, and Clouded Sky followed suit. Iron Maiden passed him the reins and went ahead, leading them further up the path with her fingers trailing along the rock wall on her right hand. The next bend in the road was sharper and narrower than ever before, the path almost impossible to see. Iron Maiden turned back to him, little more than a pale glimmer in the darkness.

"Do you have your sword?"

He did not understand why he would need his sword now, but he reached down and loosened the catch anyway.

She smiled at him and turned sharply, as if about to walk directly into the cliff. When he followed, however, he found himself walking in at the entrance to a cave.

"Heroine?"

A whisper came out of the dark.

"Take hold of my sash, *dage*. I don't want to lose you."

It wasn't proper to take her hand before he had spoken to a matchmaker, but as he reached out cautiously to take the end of her sash, their fingers brushed.

It was impossible to see anything. For a moment, neither of them spoke. Then Iron Maiden's hand retreated. Her voice sounded wistful.

"I don't know if we will survive this, *dage*, but thank you for believing me. Thank you for coming."

In the close stillness of the cave, there was no sound but the fluting of the wind outside, and a drip-drop of water from the rocks like the chimes of a bell. Clouded Sky closed his eyes. It made no difference; the dark was so absolute. But it seemed easier to speak that way.

"Heroine, with everything that has happened... I don't know if I'm worthy. I don't know if I am the hero you need."

She sighed, a wisp of breath in the dark.

"But you're the hero I have. You learned what I had to teach. You came to find me when I was captured. You fought for me when no one else had the courage. Have courage now."

At first, he'd been a little frightened of her. Then she'd become his ally, someone he could rely on. And now...

His hand clenched on her sash with the effort of restraining his feelings, and he took a deep breath to steady himself.

"You're the one who gives me courage, *meimei*. Thank

134

you."

She was so close that he could practically feel her heartbeat.

"*Dage*," she breathed. His heart bounded with hope.

"Yes?"

"You're pulling on my sash."

He drew back in embarrassment, loosening his grip, and Iron Maiden became no more than a movement on the end of her sash, a voice in the darkness.

"You are a righteous hero, Clouded Sky. You have a vanquish-dragons-and-subdue-tigers ability, a contain-the-river-and-embrace-the-ocean vision. I think that for you, Princess Morning Light will awake." A deep intake of breath, not entirely steady. "Please…please don't call me 'little sister.'"

The cave suddenly seemed very cold. Had he misjudged? Iron Maiden had told Harmonious Virtue that perhaps an attachment to something outside oneself could wake an enlightened one from mediation. Did she think he was destined to love Morning Light?

Did she think he could forget her so quickly? Iron Maiden shuffled nervously in the dark.

"Come, hero." She tugged at her sash, and Clouded Sky followed.

For a long time, they walked in silence. At first the ground was stony and uneven, but soon it became smooth and chiselled under their feet. At first there came a soft sound of water dripping inside the cave, but soon it became a trickle, and then a chattering murmur beside them.

They must have walked for hours: Iron Maiden and himself, with Flying Crane behind them. At last when it seemed they would walk blindly forever with the sound of water their only companion, a dim light began to pierce the darkness. Gradually it came closer and strengthened, until finally Clouded Sky recognised it for the grey light of dawn, shining in through an opening in the rock ahead of them.

Iron Maiden lifted a finger to her lips, and motioned to Clouded Sky to leave Flying Crane tethered to a ring in the wall. Softly, they stole closer to the cave's mouth. Iron Maiden lifted her palms warily. Sensing her nervousness, Clouded Sky drew his sword.

The air hissed. Iron Maiden spun, catching a hidden projectile in her fingers.

"The Thorns," she gasped, but her cry was choked off as more projectiles flew from all directions. Clouded Sky lifted his sword in a futile attempt to block them. Unerringly aimed, they thudded into acupoints all over his body.

He fell into a dream of pain.

* * *

It felt as though he was being systematically beaten. Expert fingers jabbed, prodded, pinched and knuckled him.

With each blow his *qi* flowed more freely, relieving the pain of closed acupoints. When they finished, Clouded Sky ached all over, but he was awake again.

Hands plucked him from the dirt and yanked him to his knees. Clouded Sky's head rolled back on his shoulders. Looking up, he saw Ten Thousand Thorns Temple.

Remote and peaceful, it perched on a ledge halfway up the mountainside, its walls and roof just a glimpse of red, grey and green among the pines. A narrow path, overgrown with weeds, ran up the eastern side of the valley to meet it.

A broad finger and thumb grabbed and pinched an acupoint on the side of his neck, causing Clouded Sky to gasp with pain.

"Stinking spy! Keep your eyes on the ground!"

Clouded Sky bent his head, but not before scanning his surroundings. He was kneeling in the street of a village tucked into a fold of the mountains, a deep gash of fruitful green among snowy peaks. Before him, steps climbed to a sturdy village hall fashioned from immense pine beams. All around clustered a wide-eyed crowd of villagers. From their murmured comments, it seemed some of them were looking at a traveller from the outside world for the very first time.

Beside Clouded Sky, two of the villagers bent over what seemed to be a shapeless bundle of clothing, jabbing and pinching. With the release of her last acupoint, Iron Maiden jerked upwards, palms flying, feet kicking. She knocked one of the villagers unconscious with a fast strike, but the other dodged and put up his fists.

"Traitor!" he growled.

She launched herself forward, her palms sweeping up dust, and her face contorted in a howl of defiance. Clouded Sky thought to twist himself from the grip his two guards kept on his shoulders, but no sooner did he tense than one of them subdued him with a heavy blow that put him back in the dust.

Coughing, he peeled his face out of the dirt and looked up. Iron Maiden aimed a storm of terrible blows at her enemy. Palms, fists, and feet moved like lightning, but each blow was blocked. The villager facing her didn't even seem concerned. Before Clouded Sky could regain his breath, Iron Maiden's opponent swept out a leg. Then, as she flipped in the air to avoid him, already he was up again and pounded both fists down on her body.

Iron Maiden hit the ground. The villager spat.

"Now you will face judgement, Nameless Girl!"

A groan escaped her. Clouded Sky couldn't believe his eyes. It had happened so fast. *So* fast. Until now, it had always taken multiple opponents to overpower Iron Maiden. Whoever these villagers were, they must be peerless martial artists, so advanced they made even Iron Maiden look like an acolyte.

"Heroine," he breathed. "Who *are* these people?"

Despite her grimace of pain, he thought she might be smiling.

138

"These are the Ten Thousand Thorns, *dage*."

"The *what?*" Clouded Sky blinked. *These* were the Ten Thousand Thorns? *Morning Light sleeps in the mountains, surrounded by ten thousand thorns.*

His skin went cold. No wonder she'd been looking for a great martial hero. And now he had failed her.

"Heroine, you didn't tell me they were martial artists!"

"Why, what did you think they were?"

"I was imagining a hedge!"

She lifted her eyebrows.

"A tremendous, *deadly* hedge!"

"Silence!" shouted the villager who had just subdued Iron Maiden.

Down the steps of the hall stalked a stocky, grizzled man gripping Clouded Sky's own sword in his fist. Clouded Sky felt the killing aura even before he saw the man's face.

"Nameless Girl." The man faced Iron Maiden in a calm white fury. "Traitor."

"Chief Valuable Ox." She smiled hopefully at him. "I returned to warn you, Elder! The Vastly Martial Emperor has sent an Imperial Sword to find Ten Thousand Thorns Temple and seize the Golden Phoenix Sword."

Valuable Ox paid no attention to her words.

"Who is this man? You know our rules. No stranger enters the valley on pain of death. No one disturbs the meditations of Princess Morning Light." He extended the sword, pointing it directly at the kneeling girl. "No one has ever dared it and lived. Except *you*, Nameless Girl."

"The Imperial Sword—" Iron Maiden began, but Valuable Ox cut through her words.

"This stranger will tell me all I need to know. But by the laws of this village, your life is doubly forfeit."

The sword flickered.

"*No!*" Clouded Sky surged forward, but he was too securely held.

Valuable Ox plunged the sword into Iron Maiden's heart.

"No!" Clouded Sky yelled again. Iron Maiden made a small, soft sound, and with it, blood flowed from her mouth. For a moment she stared up at the temple, her teeth reddened behind parted lips, her eyes glazing.

With a sigh she fell back, but even as her body fell, it rippled in the air and dissolved into a vapour. A breath of wind arose, dissipating the smoke, leaving nothing but one silken strand of black hair twisting in the breeze. Even as Clouded Sky watched, it divided into two parts as if cut by an invisible knife.

Clouded Sky reached out, and the hair drifted into his hand.

In his numb grief he heard his own voice say, *I don't know if I'm worthy. I don't know if I am the hero you need.*

And he wasn't.

But you're the hero I have. Have courage now.

All around him, the Thorns stood frozen in amazement. Then Valuable Ox dropped the sword as if it had bitten

140

him. Someone wailed, "Sorcery!"

The hands on his shoulders went slack. Clouded Sky swallowed a sob and dived forward to scoop up his black sword. There was not even a drop of blood on the blade. He didn't understand it, but neither did the Ten Thousand Thorns. Before any of them thought to move, Clouded Sky gained his feet and rampaged toward the stunned Valuable Ox, his voice boiling and breaking in his throat.

Valuable Ox's eyes widened and he threw himself aside. Clouded Sky caught him with a slashing blow, but did not stay to fight. He made a desperate leap—and in just one bound, landed on the roof of the village hall. Below, the Thorns recovered their wits with shouts of outrage. The wind hissed. Clouded Sky turned. His sword formed a flashing shield, protecting him from the Thorns' wrath even as he flung himself backward toward the overgrown path towards the abandoned temple. Morning Light was his only hope now.

As the Thorns employed their lightness skill to come after him, Clouded Sky turned and leaped from the hall's roof.

He understood now. He wasn't the hero Iron Maiden needed or deserved. She had always known that. Yet she had brought him here anyway, no matter how unworthy he was, because he was all she had.

He'd failed her in so many ways already. He couldn't fail her again.

It was time to forget his unworthiness and put all his

reliance in Heaven.

* * *

Clouded Sky's resolve fuelled his strength. In one leap he soared from the ridge-pole of the village hall to the branches of the pine-trees on the slope beyond. With only the lightest brush of his feet against the needles he shot ever higher up the face of the hill, rising like a gushing fountain or a flying lantern. The villagers fell behind him, so far that their Ten Thousand Thorns Projectiles could no longer reach him. In another moment he floated, light as thistledown, to the temple steps.

The temple was older and more ornate than the village hall. On each side of the steps a stone lion roared its warning. A portico extended from the front of the building, with its double roof turned up at the corners and topped by golden phoenixes. Against the black paint of the facade were painted golden words, silver dragons, green ribbons and red posts. Despite the temple's age, each colour was fresh and bright.

Under the shadow of the portico, however, the double doors were closed and barred with ancient timber which the passing of years had almost fused with the doors behind. Clouded Sky hesitated only a moment before smashing the bar in two with one flashing blow of his sword.

It was dim inside the temple. The windows had been

boarded up to prevent anyone from peering in, so the only light came from lamps set in ranks against the far wall before the faces of the gods. The villagers must come in by a secret entrance to feed the lamps, Clouded Sky realised, but there was no sound of any movement in the shadows.

Silhouetted against the lamplight was a small black figure.

Conscious of the Thorns hastening up the mountain on his trail, Clouded Sky sheathed his sword and hurried forward. Closer, the silhouette proved to be a small, delicate figure clad in stiff robes of yellow silk brocade. Across her knees she gripped the sheath and hilt of a sword with a golden tassel. An intricately-worked golden phoenix crown, dripping with ornaments, partly concealed her face.

Despite his danger, Clouded Sky could not bring himself to speak or move for a moment. It was true. Somehow, even though he'd staked his life on it, the fact that it was true still amazed him.

But there was no time to lose. The Thorns were on his trail.

"Princess?" It was like speaking to a doll. "Princess, of a thousand years," he tried again, a little more respectfully, and a little louder.

Still, nothing.

"Princess, I've come from Wudang Mountain. We need you. We need the Heaven-Relying Dragon-Slaying Sword

Skill. A new emperor has arisen to crush All-Under-Heaven beneath his feet. They say he has the Mandate of Heaven, and yet..." he sighed. "Princess, he does injustice and oppresses the needy. I want a better future for my people than this."

Was that a sound outside the door? He fell to his knees beside the still golden figure. "Princess, can you hear me?" and in sheer desperation he grabbed her by both shoulders and shook her.

With a discordant chime the golden crown fell to the floor.

He was afraid of what he would see. A shrivelled corpse? A wax effigy? Nothing prepared him for the reality.

Long black hair combed smooth as silk and pinned up in an intricate series of jewelled knots. A face as delicate as jade. Lips that, even in deep meditation, had something like a smile in their corners.

All of it a sight as familiar to him as his own sword.

"Heroine!"

He did not stop to think, to ask why or how. When he touched her cheeks, her skin was warm. Alive.

"*Meimei*," he whispered, and kissed her on the lips.

Under his hands her shoulders tensed. He pulled back and opened his eyes to meet her startled gaze. Then, in the corner of his eye, the lamplight leaped and flickered with the strength of a sudden killing aura.

"*Meimei*, wait—"

Shinggggg! The Golden Phoenix Sword flashed in the candlelight. The wooden sheath, thrown across the room, struck the wall as two wrathful eyes narrowed at him over the sharpest edge he'd ever seen.

"Who *dares!*"

Clouded Sky recoiled, throwing up pleading hands.

"Princess-of-a-thousand-years! Forgive me! I was sent to wake you. We need your help!" He pressed his forehead against the floor, closed his eyes, and waited for the killing blow.

It never came.

"You woke me?" Her voice was doubtful.

Clouded Sky glanced up. Morning Light touched her fingers to her cheek, then looked about her, her mouth opening in amazement.

"You woke me," she repeated. "I am home!"

There was no time to say more. Suddenly, the lamplight danced again, twisting and writhing as if in a strong wind. The Golden Phoenix stabbed toward him. Clouded Sky flinched.

Pinggggg! A hidden projectile skipped off the slender blade. The Golden Phoenix rang like a bell, one melodious note resounding through the temple as Morning Light rose from her seat and turned.

Clouded Sky looked toward the door.

The Thorns clustered on the steps of the temple blocking the doorway and the pale morning light. One young man stood paralysed in fright, his arm still extended

145

with the Flying Thorn projectile pipe visible inside his sleeve. When Morning Light turned toward them, there fell an awful silence, followed by murmurs and gasps of recognition. Then, one by one, they fell to their knees and began to kowtow. One of them cupped his fists and addressed the princess.

"Honoured lady, we have failed to protect you! Please allow us to take vengeance on this stranger before you destroy us."

Morning Light didn't reply at once. Instead, she turned to look down at Clouded Sky. Her voice was clear and brittle in the vast expanse of the temple.

"Who are you, stranger?"

Clouded Sky swallowed an aching lump in his throat.

"Honoured lady, you really don't remember me?"

A tiny line appeared between her eyebrows as she looked down at him with evident distaste.

"No. Should I?"

Then she truly was dead. Iron Maiden, his little sister. He swallowed again, and clenched his hand on the severed hair he held.

"My name is Clouded Sky," he said huskily. "I'm... " Not a Wudang Sect disciple. Not any more. "I'm nobody in particular."

"I see." Morning Light's eyes narrowed. Then she turned her sword point-down and cupped her fists, bowing. "For a hundred years I have waited for the one who would end my meditations. Morning Light thanks

146

you, hero."

"Princess!" one of the Thorns objected. "He has trespassed in the valley! He has seriously wounded Chief Valuable Ox!

"If Chief Valuable Ox was any use to me at all, he would have woken me long ago. Give this man anything he wants and send him on his way." Morning Light turned toward the door.

"Thousand-years lady, wait!" Clouded Sky leaped to his feet. "I came to ask for your help!"

Morning Light didn't look back.

"My help?"

"The Heaven-Relying Dragon-Slaying Sword Skill." Clouded Sky clasped his hands in petition. "A new emperor has arisen in Nanjing. He sends his armies to subdue All-Under-Heaven, and none can resist him! I have come all the way from Hubei to beg your help, heroine."

"The Heaven-Relying Dragon-Slaying Sword Skill?" Morning Light laughed. "That is a secret which belongs only to my family! If you think I will let any passing vagabond have it, you are mistaken!"

Clouded Sky's heart sank even further. Not only was this princess not Iron Maiden, she was not even like her. He had to struggle to keep his voice calm as he spoke.

"Before his death, I was the military aide to Duke Roaring Tiger, whose army waits on Mount Jing to face the Vastly Martial Emperor's onslaught. If we do not

147

have help, Mount Jing will fall and all of Hubei will be subjected to the emperor's rule. Sichuan will be next. Please, if you will not teach me your martial arts, then come and help us in Hubei."

Morning Light considered his words for a moment, but gave a decided shake of her head.

"My father died embroiling himself in struggles beyond the valley, and he left his people leaderless! I cannot repeat his mistakes. I cannot afford to make enemies."

Clouded Sky groaned.

"What good is it if you return from your sojourn in Heaven, heroine, only to shut yourself away in this valley?"

"Who are you to question my decisions, stranger? I was advised by those wiser than myself!"

This was exactly what the Coiling Dragon King had been afraid of. Clouded Sky shook his head in desperation.

"Thousand-years lady, you said you'd reward me! I woke you from your meditations! Your people killed my friend!"

"Killed your friend?" Morning Light turned to the villagers. "What is this?"

"It was the Nameless Girl! She wanted to wake you from your meditations!"

"I *wished* to be woken from my meditations! Who was this Nameless Girl?"

Only one of the guards was brave enough to answer

her.

"Honoured lady, we don't know who she was, but she looked just like you. She appeared in the valley half a year ago and tried to reach the Temple. We fought her and she fled. Then this morning she came back, bringing this man with her. She had broken our laws twice."

"So you killed her."

"She must have been a demon. Or a ghost! When Valuable Ox killed her, she vanished!"

Morning Light turned back to Clouded Sky, more curious now than dismissive.

"*Was* she a ghost?"

He shook his head. "I don't know what she was. Not even she knew that. But this is all that's left of her." He held out the black hair, blinking back tears.

Morning Light stepped closer and took the hair from Clouded Sky's hand. As she looked at it, her eyes widened.

But there was no time to speak again. Panicked footsteps hurtled up the path from the village, and everyone heard the voice of a young boy shouting.

"Help! Help! Enemies in the village!"

* * *

The Imperial Sword surveyed Ten Thousand Thorns Village with grim satisfaction. Despite the darkness, Second Brother had led them unerringly through the mountains on Flying Crane's trail. Better yet, the village was almost deserted when they arrived. Only a handful of the oldest and youngest inhabitants remained in their houses whilst everyone else had gone up to the temple.

After the many battles he'd fought since leaving Nanjing, the Imperial Sword had only thirty guards with him. Despite their numbers they had subdued the feeble handful of villagers, locked them into the village hall, and barricaded the door with heaps of pine boughs and straw. Now, four of his men stood before the hall with flaming torches, waiting for orders to burn the structure and everyone inside.

He'd purposefully allowed one of the young boys to escape in order to warn the others. Now Imperial Sword stood on the steps in front of the hall shading his eyes against the morning sunlight and praying that the rest of the village would see reason. Given that he was under orders to kill their princess, he doubted it.

The boy's thin cry of warning drifted down from the hillside. The Imperial Sword put his hand to his sword before remembering that the blade was broken, sliced in half by Clouded Sky at Wudang. Instead he reached under his cloak and checked that his spare weapon was safe and accessible. It was time.

He faced the temple among the pines and shouted: "Clouded Sky! Iron Maiden!"

A woman in a gold brocaded gown appeared on the edge of the cliff above him. The sword in her right hand caught the morning light like a white-hot flame reflected.

"Morning Light," he breathed in awe.

Beside him, Second Brother tensed. The Imperial Sword grabbed his shoulder.

"Remember what we agreed," he growled. "We do this my way."

He was grateful for the mask he wore. Each time he confronted Second Brother he saw a multitude of questions crossing the bounty hunter's face. Who was this Imperial Sword? How dangerous? So far, Second Brother had always chosen to put discretion before valour. Now he nodded sourly and dropped his arm.

"Your way, your excellency."

On the hillside, the princess was now joined by a crowd of people: the other villagers. With them was a man whom he recognised as Clouded Sky. There was no sign of Iron Maiden, but it was too late to worry about her now.

"Princess! Clouded Sky! Come down alone, or we will burn your people alive!"

At once the princess lifted her arms and stepped from the cliff. Clouded Sky followed her. Imperial Sword's scalp prickled as he watched the princess fly down, sword extended, golden robes rippling as though she was a phoenix herself. She took the whole drop in one soaring leap and landed on the steps of the hall facing him and Second Brother. Upon seeing her face, the Imperial Sword recoiled a step.

"Iron Maiden!"

"You seem frightened. Why is that, I wonder?" She smiled grimly, looking down her golden blade toward him.

"Who led you here? How dare you threaten my people?"

"Thousand-years lady." Clouded Sky had taken the drop from the hillside in a series of shorter leaps, and now landed breathlessly by her side. "This is—"

"I can see who it is," she interrupted. "I said, who led you here?"

Was this really Morning Light? Or just a clever impersonation by Iron Maiden? No time to ask. Imperial Sword pointed to Clouded Sky.

"This one led me here. We followed you up the mountain and through the cave."

"And took my people hostage?" Morning Light took a stance, and the guards who held torches at the hall doors tensed.

The Imperial Sword raised a hand. "Wait! Princess, I have no wish to burn your people. Let us come to an agreement."

Clouded Sky cleared his throat and stepped forward, holding out his sword hilt-first. "If it's my fault that you are here, then let me put it right. There's a price on my head. Take it and let these people go."

"No agreements!" Morning Light shouted.

"No," the Imperial Sword agreed. "We don't need you, hero, we need the Golden Phoenix. Give us the sword, princess, and we'll leave in peace."

There was a moment's silence. Under the pines on the hill, the Thorns edged closer and waited. Morning Light smiled down the edge of her blade.

"Give you the sword? Never! You'll have to kill us all first." She stepped forward. "Thorns!"

Second Brother took a stance. The guards' torches wavered, ready to set fire to the hall. The rest of the guards drew their weapons as Clouded Sky grabbed his sword. Battle loomed, but the Imperial Sword stretched out his arms like a wall between his own men and his enemies.

"No! Wait!"

All eyes stared at him. In the silence, the Imperial Sword swallowed. What could he do? Despite his bluff, there was no way he would set fire to the hall. He might be forced to kill Morning Light, but he was under no orders to slaughter the villagers.

That left only one option. The very last resort.

Slowly, still holding up a cautioning hand, he reached under his cloak and drew forth his spare weapon. Clouded Sky's mouth dropped open as he saw the broken spear of his dead blood brother. Then he flushed with rage.

"Thief! How dare you! Where did you get that?"

"At Wudang." For the first time in months, the Imperial Sword used his real voice, not the rasping whisper he'd adopted to disguise it. "I took it from your old room, *shidi.*"

"*Shidi?*" Clouded Sky repeated in shock. *Martial younger brother.* "No…"

Broken Spear peeled the fabric mask from his face and faced his blood brother with quiet resolve.

"Am I a thief, Clouded Sky? I only took what was my own."

* * *

Heaven and earth stood still. Clouded Sky stared in horror.

After a moment, Morning Light stamped her foot and cried, "Enough talk! Release my people, or eat my sword!"

As she tensed to spring, Clouded Sky threw himself in front of her with his arms outstretched.

"Princess, no! Please! It's my blood brother."

Morning Light's eyes widened, so that she looked very much like Iron Maiden indeed.

"*This—?*"

Clouded Sky turned to face the Imperial Sword. For a long, awful moment he searched the other man's face.

"Tell me it's not true," he whispered at last. "Please, tell me this is not what it appears to be."

For one brief heartbeat, Broken Spear dropped his gaze. It was little more than a flicker of the eyes, but it told Clouded Sky everything he needed to know. The knowledge was far worse than thinking his martial elder brother, his *shige,* was simply dead.

"You know me, *shidi*," Broken Spear began.

"I thought I did! Was I wrong?"

"There's a reason for my actions."

His actions. Like holding these villagers hostage. Like what he had done to Iron Maiden. Like choosing to serve the Emperor at all. Clouded Sky stepped back, lifting his sword.

"Why? We fought the Emperor together, *shige!*"

"He offered me a pardon. My freedom…"

"Your *freedom?* What kind of freedom comes through terrorising and tormenting innocent people? What about peace? What about All-Under-Heaven crying out for relief? You were the one who taught me to care for those things, *shige!*"

"I still do!" Broken Spear cried the words like one goaded beyond bearing. "How can you think I would betray that dream?"

"Because you have betrayed everything else!" Morning Light burst out.

"The ultimate goal for a warrior is to put his sword aside," Broken Spear continued. "The ultimate purpose of war is peace. It was as I meditated upon this truth that I was enlightened, and much became clear to me. I realised why we need the Vastly Martial Emperor."

Clouded Sky shook his head mutely.

"All-Under-Heaven is filled with suffering, with division, with chaos. Because of division, there is war. Because of war, there is suffering. But the Vastly Martial

155

Emperor will bring unity. There will be no more war. There will be no more famine. No more families torn apart, no more homes burned down. *Peace.*"

"Peace?!" Morning Light stamped her foot.

She might have gone on, but Broken Spear bowed to her.

"The Vastly Martial Emperor understands the necessity of mercy. Give up the Golden Phoenix and swear allegiance! All your people will be spared."

"Sooner than live a slave, I and my people will die fighting! Better to be broken jade than unharmed brick!"

"Clouded Sky, *shidi!*" Broken Spear pleaded. "Help me to reason with her!"

Clouded Sky gasped for breath. His chest felt as though it was bound with iron; he thought the air would explode from tension. His Wudang Sect Elders had declared that they must endure the Vastly Martial Emperor, but Broken Spear had determined to join him. Morning Light moved restlessly. Clouded Sky put up a hand to hold her back.

"Honoured lady, wait. He's right. We must end this with as little bloodshed as possible."

"What?" Her knuckles whitened on her sword-hilt. "Give him what he wants? Never!"

Clouded Sky shook his head.

"No. But if there's going to be fighting, that's my duty. I brought him here, after all."

She stared at him for a moment, and then, in acknowledgement, lowered her sword.

"A duel!"

Broken Spear started. "*Shidi*, no! You're no match for me!"

"I know, *shige*. I'm no great hero." Clouded Sky smiled calmly. "That's why I'm going to fight you."

* * *

They marked off a space in the village square. Broken Spear gave leave for twenty of the Thorns to descend from the cliffs as a guard for Clouded Sky and Morning Light. Together with the imperial guards, these formed the ring in which Broken Spear and Clouded Sky faced each other. Only the torchbearers on the steps of the hall kept their posts.

At the centre of the ring of warriors, Clouded Sky transferred his sword from palm to palm as Broken Spear twirled his truncated spear and took a stance. Morning Light's golden sleeves floated in the wind as she held the Golden Phoenix like a bar between them.

"This is a duel to the death," she announced. "If Clouded Sky kills Imperial Sword, the guards will surrender and my people will conduct them out of my realm. None will ever return on pain of instant death! If Imperial Sword kills Clouded Sky, then the Golden Phoenix Sword will be handed over to him." She lifted her chin proudly. "But my people will never, never submit to the Vastly Martial Emperor! Not while the Coiling Dragon King's daughter

157

still lives! Begin!"

She struck the ground with her foot and soared backwards out of the circle, leaving the two combatants to face each other.

Clouded Sky adopted a stance. Broken Spear looked at him sadly.

"*Shidi*, I don't want to kill you."

"You leave me no choice, brother! If I don't fight you like this, then what happens? Will you burn these people alive?"

A hot denial rose to Broken Spear's lips, but he forced it back. How could he say it? If he admitted that he would never kill the villagers, then he might as well surrender now and cut his own throat before the Emperor did it for him.

He knew what his reasoning boiled down to: Better that Clouded Sky should die rather than the villagers. Better that the villagers should die rather than himself and his men.

Second Brother was right: there was no way to serve this Emperor and remain a righteous man.

He ought to have known. He ought to have done anything rather than stand here preparing to kill his blood brother so that he could save his own neck.

When did he become such a coward?

Clouded Sky attacked first in a low, furious lunge. Broken Spear launched himself into the air, avoiding Clouded Sky's blade and stabbing toward his head with the half-spear. In the blink of an eye, without warning, Clouded Sky changed direction. His sword-strike was powerful enough to create a howling wind as he swung it.

Boom!

It met the steel-sheathed haft of the spear with an explosion of energy that blew both of them several paces back. They circled warily. Broken Spear could see that the fight was not truly on Clouded Sky's mind—but when the question came, he was unprepared.

"Did you betray Roaring Tiger to the emperor, *shige?*"

Broken Spear swallowed.

"Roaring Tiger brought grief and trouble to all of Hubei."

The colour drained from Clouded Sky's face; the tip of his sword trembled.

"So you turned him over to the Emperor?"

"I was sure he would see reason!" Once, Broken Spear had thought it would be impossible to make this confession, but in this moment it came to him as a relief. A chance to justify himself. "The Emperor offered Roaring Tiger the same terms he offered me, but he was too stubborn to accept them. It is because of men like him that All-Under-Heaven is in the trouble it is today!"

"It is because of men like *you* that the Emperor has any power at all!" Once again, Clouded Sky launched forward. Under the intensity of his furious attack, Broken Spear was forced back across the ring, unable to do anything but defend. Clouded Sky's martial arts were not as polished as his own, but they held a raw, unpredictable force that was new to him. At last, just as the guards began to give way behind Broken Spear, he saved himself with a wild leap, soaring over Clouded Sky's head. The black sword slashed. Broken Spear landed on his feet, but there was a gash across his left forearm. First blood.

Morning Light and the Thorns cheered.

Broken Spear backed away. One of his guards offered him a strip of cloth to bind the wound, and within a few seconds he had knotted the bandage tight with his teeth.

"You would have trusted me once, *shidi*. You would have believed that my heart was honest."

Clouded Sky looked wretched. "Have you behaved like an honest man?"

"I have tried to do the right thing. I knew the emperor's men were ruthless, and I have always done what I could to mitigate their cruelty. I would not let them lay a hand on Iron Maiden. I kept her alive."

"You kept her chained in a cage like a beast. Sick, starving, thirsting, in agony!"

"I did her as little harm as I could!"

"But you did not have the courage to do justice!"

Clouded Sky moved with devastating force and speed. "For Roaring Tiger!"

The force of his blow, though Broken Spear blocked it, was bone-shattering. It tossed him across the ring like a leaf on the wind.

"For Iron Maiden!"

Three strikes of the sword and Broken Spear fell to the ground, clutching a pierced acupoint on his thigh.

"For All-Under-Heaven!"

And Clouded Sky stabbed down toward his friend's heart.

* * *

Shing!

With one last panicked motion Broken Spear managed to deflect the blow. Instead of cleaving his heart the black sword sank into his shoulder, pinning him to the ground. As a line of red welled up around the blade, all the madness went out of Clouded Sky, leaving him shaking and sweating, cold with horror.

Broken Spear gave a soft groan of pain as Clouded Sky yanked his sword out and staggered back, sickened as though the wound was his own.

"Tell your men to quench their torches and surrender. Then go and never return. Or I *will* kill you."

Broken Spear seemed to shrink in on himself with shame. Then he turned onto his elbow and looked at his guards.

"Do as he says."

The guards hesitated. One of them dropped his torch on the ground, but Second Brother did neither. Instead, his hands dipped to his waist and then flung out.

Morning Light gave an exclamation and leaped into the air. *Shingg!* The Golden Phoenix swept aside a flying dagger. *Thunk!* A second passed harmlessly under her feet and sank into the wall of the house behind her.

A third embedded itself deep in her shoulder. A fourth, in her stomach. They had flown so fast that no one saw them, not even the princess. Morning Light staggered a little, staring down at them in shocked surprise.

Already Second Brother held new daggers in his hands, ready to throw again.

"Stand your ground!" he shouted to the other guards. "The golden witch must die and her sword taken to Nanjing. Those were the Emperor's orders!"

"Second Brother! No!" Broken Spear lifted a shaking hand. "We had an agreement!"

Second Brother smiled ruthlessly; Clouded Sky sensed the malice of his killing aura like a desert wind or a dragon's breath.

"Did I say my name was Second Brother? I lied! I am Snow Wind, the Emperor's commissioner! Already my Venomous Knives spread poison through the witch's veins. Now give up the sword!"

Morning Light's mouth firmed. She wrapped her fingers around the dagger-hilts and grunted as she drew them out. The wounds bubbled as, with an exertion of her *qi* energy, she expelled the poison from her blood.

Snow Wind's mouth dropped open.

"Thorns!" cried Morning Light. "Attack!"

At once her twenty Thorns charged the Emperor's guards. More Thorns leaped from their hiding-places among the roofs and walls of the village; others soared down from the hillside. Snow Wind swore and threw his daggers. Snatching a torch from the guard beside him, he thrust it into the bales of hay that surrounded the hall. Morning Light shouted and lifted her sword to defend herself, but Snow Wind's flying daggers never reached her.

At Clouded Sky's feet, Broken Spear coughed blood as the four daggers thudded home in his body.

"*Shige!*" Clouded Sky fell to his knees.

Flames roared as they took hold of the village hall. For a moment the Thorns were in chaos, as all of them raced to unbar the doors and rescue their oldest parents and youngest children. In the confusion, the imperial guards attacked, killing a few. Then, quickly, the Thorns rallied. A small band joined battle while the others fetched water or blankets to smother the flames.

In front of the hall, Morning Light screamed like a bird of prey and launched herself at Snow Wind.

Among all the warriors of the martial arts world, Snow Wind was ranked among the five greatest. Not a flicker of nervousness crossed his face as the vengeful princess descended upon him. Instead, he loosed his remaining daggers toward her and drew his paired hooks as she swatted the Venomous Knives aside.

Then they met. Snow Wind stomped forward trying

163

to catch the supple Golden Phoenix between his hooks and snap the blade. Morning Light fought like a dragon flying or a phoenix dancing, striking glancing blows, never staying in one place long enough to be caught. The pair looked like the boiling clouds of a thunderstorm, black and flashing with gold, employing not just weapons but also fingers, palms, fists, and feet. The energy their weapons possessed sparked with each blow.

Lying in Clouded Sky's arms, Broken Spear watched them with glazing eyes.

"The Heaven-Relying Dragon-Slaying Sword Skill," he breathed. "At last! I see it with my own eyes!"

Clouded Sky blinked back his tears. Even as he watched, the Golden Phoenix danced and flickered like a tongue of lightning, its every motion causing it to thrum with a sweet and deadly melody. Step by step, the princess forced Snow Wind to retreat. As powerful and unorthodox as his martial arts were, he was no match for Morning Light.

Clouded Sky jumped as Broken Spear's bloody hand clutched at his neck. The wounded man's fingers tightened and dragged him down, eye to fading eye. Broken Spear stared at the duel, his whole body trembling, his voice the thinnest of whispers.

"*I was wrong, shidi!*"

Gently, Clouded Sky tried to loosen Broken Spear's grip. "Lie back, martial brother! Don't waste your strength!"

Broken Spear only gripped harder.

"I should have relied on Heaven," he rasped. "But I was too afraid. Look where it has brought me! Don't—don't—be afraid—*shidi*."

A spasm passed through him. All his muscles contracted, pulling Clouded Sky into one final, involuntary embrace. Then he fell back in Clouded Sky's arms.

"*Shige!* No!" Frantically, Clouded Sky shook the body. "Don't leave me again!"

But there was no reply.

* * *

A familiar voice reached him.

"Clouded Sky *dage!* Quick! *Lu Dongbin Pierces the Dragon!*"

The words jolted him out of his grief. His sword lay on the ground beside him. He grabbed it without questioning or thinking and stabbed upward as directed.

It struck the acupoint of a guard attacking from behind. The man fell with a howl of pain.

Clouded Sky jumped to his feet and backed away as three more guards converged on him. Aside from Second Brother, still locked in his duel with Morning Light, they were the only guards remaining. Most had now surrendered or fallen, and the Thorns were now busy with the burning hall.

Exhausted by the fighting he had already done, and still

165

reeling from the shock of Broken Spear's appearance and death, Clouded Sky felt ready to give up. How could he hope to fight them all?

With a shout, they attacked.

The voice called again.

"Hero-Killing Forefinger! Roaming Wind on Rainbow Mountain! Jade Maiden Throws the Shuttle!"

Clouded Sky moved almost blindly, but each stance countered the attacks of his enemies.

"Assault on Heaven-Defying Gate! Iron Rod Breaks the Vase! Serpent-Crushing Divine Heel!"

These were stances he'd never learned. Could they be part of the Heaven-Relying Dragon-Slaying Sword Skill? But that would mean—

His heart soared with hope.

"Heroine!" Somehow, he found his rhythm. The weariness rolled away, leaving him alert and buoyant. "Heroine! Where are you?"

Morning Light laughed. The Golden Phoenix sang as she drove Snow Wind back another step. Bleeding from half a dozen wounds, the bounty hunter tripped and fell. At once he regained his feet. Snow Wind howled and attacked, but his stroke was wild and his footing unsteady. Morning Light flitted aside, and as he dashed nearer, her sword pierced him through.

Snow Wind fell into the dust beside Broken Spear, twitched, and lay still.

Clouded Sky leaped back, putting a short distance

166

between himself and the three surviving guards.

"Surrender, and your lives will be spared!"

With terrified glances at Morning Light the three men dropped their weapons. The sound of battle stilled, leaving only the dull roar of the blazing village hall. Morning Light lowered the Golden Phoenix Sword and called her people to secure the prisoners. When Clouded Sky reached her side, she stood looking down at the two dead men.

"Such a shame, *dage*. Such martial artists they were! Now they will never take disciples, and their unique techniques will die with them."

"Dage!" As much as he had lost today, he couldn't help smiling. "You remember me! And you know your martial arts!"

She gave him the smile that he remembered so well.

"Yes, I remember! I think I have dreamed of you during my meditations." She lifted her hand, and he saw that she still held the strand of black hair knotted around her fingers. "When I touch this, I remember my dreams. It seems to me that I ought to know you well."

"Then you were Iron Maiden all the time? But how?"

One of the Thorns interrupted them.

"Thousand-years lady! The hall cannot be saved, but we have prevented the fire from spreading to other houses."

"And the people?"

"Everyone is safe, my lady."

"Then let's not worry about the hall. A hall can be

rebuilt!"

"And burned down again next time the Emperor sends an Imperial Sword for you!" The voice came from behind them. Clouded Sky and Morning Light turned. Down the road that led away from the secret cave came an old woman leaning on her staff.

"Of course, if he does, you will have only yourselves to blame!" She pointed the tip of her staff at Morning Light. "You could have remained in Heaven, enjoying spiritual enlightenment, young lady! But no, you had to go and wake yourself up!"

Morning Light's eyes grew wide in recognition.

Clouded Sky stuttered, "Respected One! I know you!"

"I should think so! If it wasn't for me, you'd still be a prisoner in Wudang." She narrowed her eyes at the chaotic state of the village—the corpses of Thorns and imperial guards littering the ground, the injured folk being treated for cuts and burns, the still-burning hall and the blackened faces of the firefighters. "Seems like I ought to have been here, too! You've made a fine mess of things, haven't you?"

Morning Light waved her hand with the hair twined around the fingers. "I remember you, Elder! You were the one who did this!"

"Took one of your hairs and made a second body for you to go wandering the martial arts world in?" The old lady grimaced. "Only under protest, girl. Orders from the *highest* level. It was thought that otherwise, no worthy hero would ever stumble upon you!"

"Then it wasn't just a dream. I was really there!" Morning Light glanced sidelong at Clouded Sky. "I didn't remember who I was. But it was me, all the same."

The old lady sniffed. "Indeed."

"Thank you! Thank you!" Impulsively, Morning Light threw her arms around the old lady.

There was a flash of light. Suddenly, where there had been wrinkles and white hair, there was the smooth skin and raven hair of a young and beautiful maiden.

"How dare you? Show some respect!" she scolded. "Remember my station! Don't behave like a peasant girl!"

Morning Light laughed and backed away, cupping her fists and bowing. "Immortal Lady He, humble self thanks you a thousand times!"

"I hope you don't regret it." To Clouded Sky the immortal lady said, "You'll have to teach her some manners."

"I'd rather learn her sword skill. That is, if she'll take me as her disciple."

Immortal Lady He shrugged and gave a shrill whistle. At once there was a flash of white in the sky. A crane drifted down from its perch in the crags and landed beside her.

The lady settled herself on its back. "I'm meant to tell you that the Emperor's army is already in Hubei. Wudang Temple has refused to send help to Mount Jing, on account of their purpose of heavenly contemplation. If you want to save either of them, you'd better set out at once."

She winged away. Clouded Sky looked at Morning Light, his joy beginning to recede. How much did she remember about him, really? Did she know how he felt about her? And even if she did, was there any hope for him? It was one thing to ask for a match with Iron Maiden, nameless martial wanderer. It was another to ask for a match with the daughter of the Coiling Dragon King. Worse, if she became his *shimu*, his martial arts mother, then it was forbidden even to dream of such a thing.

"Heroine?"

She turned back to him with a smile.

"Of course we must go and help them, *dage*."

He smiled and nodded, trying not to let his doubt show in his eyes.

"And the Heaven-Relying Dragon-Slaying Sword Skill? Will you teach me?"

Morning Light looked thoughtful. Clouded Sky waited in anxious silence. If she agreed, he'd rise in the martial arts world, but he could never love her. If she refused, he would never be a great martial artist, but at least he could hope to ask for her hand one day.

"You are a quick learner, *dage*," Morning Light said at last. "Perhaps you do not need me to teach you at all." She picked up the end of her golden sash and smoothed the silk thoughtfully between her fingers. "Not many people believe it, but Coiling Dragon King did indeed leave the secrets of the Heaven-Relying Dragon-Slaying

Sword Skill written inside a secret sword manual. What do you think, *dage?* Could you learn from a book?"

Clouded Sky felt the warmth of dawning hope. "Yes, thousand-years lady! Yes, I believe I could."

"'Thousand-years lady'? So formal! When you woke me, you called me *meimei.*" She dropped her sash and turned toward the village square. "Let's find something to eat. I'm hungry!"

Clouded Sky stood for a moment staring after her. Slowly, a smile broke across his face, and he hurried to catch her up. "Wait for me, *meimei!*"

S.D.G.

About the Author

Suzannah Rowntree lives in a big house in rural Australia with her awesome parents and siblings, reading academic histories of the Crusades and writing historical fantasy fiction that blends folklore and myth with historical fact. She is the author of the historical fantasy series *Watchers of Outremer* as well as the Arthurian fantasy *Pendragon's Heir* and a series of fairytale retellings.

You can connect with me on:
- https://suzannahrowntree.site
- https://twitter.com/suzannahtweets

Subscribe to my newsletter:
- https://www.subscribepage.com/srauthor

Also by Suzannah Rowntree

The Fairy Tale Retold Series
The Rakshasa's Bride
The Prince of Fishes
The Bells of Paradise
Death Be Not Proud
Ten Thousand Thorns
The City Beyond the Glass

The Pendragon's Heir Trilogy
The Door to Camelot
The Quest for Carbonek
The Heir of Logres

The Watchers of Outremer Series
Children of the Desolate
A Wind from the Wilderness
The Lady of Kingdoms

Made in the USA
Middletown, DE
16 February 2021